DEATH AT ST PAUL'S CATHEDRAL

LONDON COSY MYSTERIES
BOOK 5

RACHEL MCLEAN

MILLIE RAVENSWORTH

This is a work of fiction. Names, characters, businesses, places, events and incidents are either the products of the author's imagination or used in a fictitious manner. Any resemblance to actual persons, living or dead, or actual events is purely coincidental.

Ackroyd Publishing

ackroyd-publishing.com

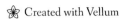

Created with Vellum

CHAPTER ONE

As she trotted down the stairs from her flat, Diana Bakewell sniffed the air. It held the delicious promise of something freshly cooked, something buttery and vanilla-scented.

Zaf Williams was by the front door, looking through today's post.

"Have you made pancakes?" she asked.

"I did," he replied. "It's our six-month anniversary. He's taking me out. What can I offer except indulgent breakfasts?"

The large house they shared in leafy Eccleston Square was divided into three flats. Zaf's boyfriend, Alexsei, owned the bottom one. He actually owned the whole building, or at least managed it on behalf of his wealthy father. Alexsei had encouraged some good habits in Zaf, not least being up early and ready for the day.

Although it was possible Zaf was simply up early in preparation for the course he was beginning at the Guild of Tourism. Perhaps he had first day nerves.

Zaf frowned at an envelope. "Who on earth is P D Bakewell? I assume that's someone you know."

"I'll deal with that," she said, taking it from him. She spotted another letter with a handwritten address on the front. "Ah."

"Ah?" said Zaf.

"This is the one I want to read. It's from Morris Walker."

Zaf frowned. "The famous criminal mastermind who bled a fortune from our company?"

Diana gave a small shake of her head. "There are things he's been accused of, but I never saw anything but kindness from the man."

"I know. Sorry." Zaf had heard the whole sorry tale before. The scandalous selling of thousands of fake tour tickets, the criminal trial and, even now, the financial hardship the bus tour company they both worked for was enduring as it tried to make good on the lost money.

"I thought I'd walk with you to college," she said, checking her watch.

"St Paul's is in absolutely the wrong direction for work."

She shrugged innocently. "I like visiting the old place. Besides, there are no tours this morning and Newton is doing something complicated with the buses. No one will mind if I stay out of the way for a while."

Zaf couldn't argue with that.

Diana suggested they walk over to Bond Street so they could travel on the Elizabeth Line. It was a bright day, the kind of day where London rose above the litter and noise and became the city she loved.

"How long will we keep calling it the 'new' Elizabeth Line?" asked Zaf as they found seats on the crowded tube train. "It's been open a few years already."

"If I know anything about people, it will be 'new' for years to come," said Diana with a wink. "It's a way to acknowledge that we remember the world when the line didn't exist."

Zaf laughed. "Like 'I knew the band before they were famous'? Yeah, I get that. Go on then, what does he say?"

"Who?"

He nodded at the letter from Morris, which Diana had already opened. "I bet it's strange getting post from a prisoner. D'you think the sniffer dogs have checked it?"

"Sniffer dogs can't read, Zaf," Diana pointed out as she scanned the sheets of paper. "Hmm, he's nearly finished the books I sent. I must get some more over to him." She caught a line on the second sheet. "I don't know how it is he finds out stuff before we do. Apparently he's heard that Chartwell and Crouch are selling off some of its assets."

"Assets?"

"That can only mean buses." There had been rumblings to that effect at work recently. Paul Kensington, the manager of the Chartwell and Crouch office in Marylebone, had been taking lots of photographs of the buses. There was always the possibility that it was a promotional exercise, to drum up more business, but Diana knew that was just wishful thinking.

"There are no other real assets," she said. "Paul Kensington has been moaning for weeks that the books won't balance. I suppose it was inevitable."

"But poor Newton. Those buses are like his babies. He'll be beside himself."

"I'm afraid he'll probably have to cope," said Diana. "It's not the end of the world. Hopefully, those old buses will go to new and loving owners. It's difficult but it's not like anyone's died."

CHAPTER TWO

Zaf stared out of the window of the tube carriage into the darkness of the tunnel, surprised that Diana had decided to accompany him to the Guild of Tourism. It was kind of her, he supposed, since it was a place she knew well, whilst he'd never been there. But the feeling persisted, the sense of being dropped off for his first day at school by a caring parent.

The Elizabeth Line carriage gleamed with newness and he enjoyed the futuristic feel of the journey. They got off at Farringdon and walked over towards St Paul's Cathedral.

"If Chartwell and Crouch don't have any buses, will we still have jobs as tour guides?" he asked. "I know we do some work that doesn't need the buses, but it's not much."

Diana shrugged. He was right. They'd managed to sign up a dozen people for the Swinging Sixties tour of London, which focused on Carnaby Street. It was a bright and breezy two hours and the tourists loved it. But the walking tours didn't bring in the money like the big bus trips.

"If Paul Kensington has ideas about the future of the company, he's not sharing them," she said. "Let's be grateful that your training's already paid for. If you do need to get another job then getting certified will make a big difference."

"Certified makes me sound insane."

"Qualified, then."

Zaf tried to picture his future as they walked along the sweeping curve of Smithfield by St Bart's Hospital . He'd always assumed it would be with Chartwell and Crouch, and more importantly with Diana and their driver Newton Crombie. Not to mention Gus the cat. When he tried to imagine himself with a different company, it was hard to summon the idea. Which other companies did he even know about? There was ACE Tours, but most of what he knew about them was that Diana had some serious beef with a woman who worked there. They had fancy new buses, not like the quirky vintage Routemasters of Chartwell and Crouch. Zaf wasn't sure if he approved.

"Hey! You're not moping, are you?" Diana asked. "Focus on what you can control right now, and that is getting your certification."

"Will do." Zaf pulled on a smile.

They cut through the narrow pedestrianised Rose Street and into spacious Paternoster Square. Despite the bold memorial column at its centre, Zaf knew the square was an almost entirely new development, a second attempt to fill a space that had been bombed during World War Two.

"Don't be surprised if there are a fair number of old people there," Diana said.

"Hmm?"

She gestured to a building beyond Temple Bar Gate leading towards the Cathedral. The Guild of Tourism.

"People grow up admiring the heritage of our city, and learn bits and pieces over the years, and then they want to formalise their skills by undertaking tour guide training," she said. "It's often volunteers from some of the historic sites."

"And those are the people who think it would be fun to spend all day long somewhere amazing like St Paul's."

St Paul's Cathedral loomed over the area. Built after the Great Fire of London, it had been the tallest building in London for over three hundred years. But its impressiveness lay in more than its size. In a country where every other church or cathedral was a set of jagged spires trying to stab the sky, St Paul's egg-like dome spoke to the soul in a different way.

"Both St Paul's and the Guild of Tourism pride themselves on being at the heart of the community," Diana said. "Some people love the Cathedral more than they love their own homes. You see it when there's a big collective loss. You're too young to remember the death of Diana, or 9/11, but this is where people gather when they want to grieve together for something huge."

"The Guild is older than St Paul's, though?"

Diana nodded. "The Guild's roots are medieval. Wren got to build this magnificent Cathedral because the Great Fire destroyed the old one. The Guild occupies even older buildings."

Zaf looked up at the building. It was made of stone and adorned with coats of arms. "It's got proper old Harry Potter windows."

"Mullion windows. You'll be expected to remember the correct terms for things when you have your certification."

"Harry Potter windows." There was a little ancient inn or house next door, squashed up next to a more modern building, and covered in scaffolding and plastic sheet screening. "Is that a Guild building or a Cathedral one?" asked Zaf.

"That's a hostel used to house some of the Cathedral's

guests. Started out as a medieval almshouse. There's a good chance some of the people on your course will be staying there. Shall we find where you need to go?"

Zaf looked at Diana. "You're coming in with me?"

She held up her hands. "Not if you don't want me to. I haven't stopped by in a while, though."

"Fine." Zaf rolled his eyes. "Let's go!"

They walked up the stone steps and through a grand wooden door. The interior was cool and dark, with flagstones underfoot. A reception area was sectioned off by a glazed partition.

"Hi," Zaf said. "I'm on the course to get my tourism badge."

"Let's get you signed in, shall we?" The woman on the other side slid a form towards Zaf. She glanced across at Diana. "Oh, Diana Bakewell! One of our old girls come back to visit."

Zaf looked up from filling in the form. "Old girl?"

"When you have gained your certification you will be an old boy, Zaf," Diana told him, then turned to the woman. "Nidra, good to see you. Tell me, did I see some building work next door?"

"Yes. The newer wing on the hostel is being refurbished. There's some fire cladding that needs to be replaced. Problem with some chemicals. Toxic apparently, although I think it sounds like it should be in your breakfast cereal."

"Diana Bakewell! What an absolute delight!"

This voice was loud, too loud for the hush of this ancient place. Zaf turned to see Ariadne Webb coming up through the entrance. Zaf gave a smile of greeting, but he knew Ariadne was the last person Diana wanted to see. The two of them had a rich and complicated history stretching back through similar tour guide careers to their days together in a pop band, and before that to childhood in London's East End. They were in many ways alike, yet the years had soured the relationship between them.

"Zaf too! You must be here for your certification. How very wonderful." Ariadne's energy made her seem a generation younger than Diana, but they were much the same age. "Jed's here doing the same thing," she continued. "Jed? Jed? Where are you?"

The young man hovering behind Ariadne gave them an awkward wave. Zaf did the same. God, it really was like the first day at school. Mums dropping their boys off and embarrassing them at the school gate. Jed gave Zaf a grin, a grin that was sly and beautiful.

"Ariadne here is an *old* girl of the Guild too. A pleasure to see you again.," said Diana.

Ariadne forced a smile. "Must be off. Tours to manage. ACE Tours is going from strength to strength." She reached out a hand, almost brushing Zaf's chest. "Maybe we'll poach this young buck, once he's qualified."

"Are we cluttering up reception and preventing the students from getting to orientation?" said a woman in formal trouser suit, approaching the quartet. Zaf recognised her. It was Carolyn Desanti, who had helped out with a mudlarking activity on the Thames foreshore when Diana and Zaf were entertaining visiting American tourists.

Ariadne smiled. "Oops. Getting into trouble with the head teacher on the first day."

"One of the lecturers," replied Carolyn. "Nothing more."

Diana eyed Zaf. "Don't believe a word of it."

"Samuel Blackthorn is about to address the new students," said Carolyn. "I could show these gentlemen the way." She looked at Diana and Ariadne. "And it's a genuine pleasure to see you. You must drop into my office for a cup of tea at some point."

Ariadne opened her mouth to speak, but Diana got there first. "I do have to pop into the depot briefly, but if you're free later..."

"Send me a text." Carolyn replied. "Zaf and... Jed, was it? This way?"

Diana grabbed Zaf. "Pay attention. Be good."

"Yes, Mum."

She couldn't help but smile.

"But pay attention to Carolyn and Dr Blackthorn. They've forgotten more about this city than even I will ever know. Truly, there's two people who know where *all* the bodies are buried."

CHAPTER THREE

Zaf sat in the Guild of Tourism assembly hall among a dozen or so other new recruits. The room was at the centre of the building, with high windows and lots of mellow wooden fittings. On a stage at one end, chairs were set out as if for formal addresses.

The school-like vibe made him uneasy.

Carolyn took her place on the stage. She was already wearing the black robe that Zaf guessed signalled she was in charge.

Jed leant towards him. "You ever been to that Harry Potter World exhibition thing?"

"Tell me about it," Zaf whispered back. "Reckon they're gonna get the Sorting Hat out in a minute?"

Most of the people in the hall were definitely middle-aged or older. The staff, too.

Doctor Samuel Blackthorn stepped up to the lectern. He was a giant bear of a man with a bushy ginger beard.

"Welcome to the Guild of Tourism," he boomed. "I always enjoy meeting a new intake. You are the lifeblood of an institution that goes back to the days of the Parish Constables in medieval times. Yes, we have our roots in a similar foundation to the police force. We safeguard the knowledge of our magnificent city, just as they keep the peace amongst its citizens." He peered around the room over the top of his glasses.

"So what can you expect from your time here? You will have three weeks of intense, world-leading learning, culminating in your final assessment. But for those of you who are successful, we expect your relationship with us to last a lifetime. Like the Cathedral that stands over us, we are a symbol of endurance through adversity. We always shine a warm and welcoming light on our city."

Carolyn stood up next.

"Today is orientation," she said. "There will be a series of lessons from myself, Dr Blackthorn and Georg Strandman. He is flying in from his missionary posting in Egypt as we speak and should be ready for you tomorrow, when your lessons will start in earnest. Today's principal activity will be a small tour, during which you will have time to mingle with your classmates and form groups. Sound good?"

A few enthusiastic 'yeah's came from the audience.

"Can you all begin by turning to the people next to you and introducing yourselves? These are your classmates."

Zaf gave Jed a daft handshake.

"Hello. I'm Zaf."

"Pleased to meet you, Zaf. I'm Jed."

"Charmed."

"Indubitably."

He turned to the woman on his other side. She was older, with strands of grey running through her black hair, and a serious look.

She smiled at him, then reached into her bag and pulled out a folded, laminated name plate: *Parvani Kadivar*.

"Zaf," Jed whispered in his ear. "Were we supposed to bring name plates?"

Parvani heard him and smiled. "Don't worry, it's only that I like to be very prepared. My name is Parvani."

"I can see that," said Zaf. "Good to, um, meet you, Parvani. Or do we call you Parv?"

She tilted her head. "I like the way that saying 'Parvani' makes people smile. It's the 'ee' sound at the end."

"That's a good reason to use your full name. I'm working as a tour guide. Just here to get certified."

"Oh, you'll be way ahead of me then. This is a change of career thing for me. Used to work as a scientist at Imperial, but I love London history."

"It's the best." Zaf gestured at Jed. "This is Jed. He's a tour guide, too. Rival company. We're like Gryffindor and Slytherin."

Jed leaned around Zaf to smile at Parvani. "I'm the Gryffindor. And this..." He motioned to the woman next to him.

In the seat beyond Jed sat one of the most powerfully-built women Zaf had ever seen. She looked to be in her fifties, but she exuded the energy of a nightclub bouncer.

"This is Josephine." Jed leant back.

Zaf held out a hand to her.

Jed gave him a warning look. "She's got a firm handshake."

The woman glared at him. Zaf withdrew his hand, wondering what the other trainees would be like.

CHAPTER FOUR

Diana decided to take the hour's walk from St Paul's to the Chartwell and Crouch bus depot in Marylebone. It was almost three miles through Holborn and along Oxford Street, but walks through her beloved city filled Diana with energy. *Use it or lose it.*

She was worried about Newton Crombie, the driver and engineer at the Chartwell and Crouch depot. The vintage Routemaster buses they used for their tours were not merely the source of his income. They were his life and soul. Despite having a large family, the buses appeared to be the true loves of his life. Diana hoped the news she'd heard from Morris was baseless gossip.

As she entered the depot there was an industrious clanking sound from the workshop.

"Newton!" called Diana. "It's only me."

Newton emerged from beneath a bus, his face covered in grease and his clothes scruffy. "Let's get the kettle on," he grinned. "I'm parched."

Diana looked him up and down. "Newton, how long have you been here this morning?"

"Been here since yesterday," he said. "Some maintenance needed doing."

Newton wasn't meeting Diana's eye. This wasn't unusual – the man wasn't exactly a people person, and the lack of sleep would account for him being even gruffer than usual. But it was hard not to suspect he was up to something.

"What maintenance are you doing?" she asked. "It must be pretty urgent if you were here all night."

"The engine bays need painting," said Newton as he filled the kettle.

"So you've taken the engine blocks out of both buses?" asked Diana.

Newton nodded. "Gus has been helping. Mostly by somehow sitting on the exact spanner that I need at any given point in time."

Gus the depot cat appeared on cue, jumping onto a vacant chair and making his small chirrup of greeting to show he was available for fuss.

"I received a letter this morning," Diana said. "From Morris Walker."

Newton paused in the act of making tea to look at her. "You're still in touch with him?"

"I am."

She could understand his suspicion. Everyone had dealt with the news about Morris in different ways. Long before Zaf had joined the company, Newton and Diana had known Morris as a supportive and caring depot manager. Diana had known him even longer, from their days in the music biz. He had an avuncular manner that matched his round and cuddly appearance. People had loved Morris.

And then tragedy had struck. Thousands of customers had been fleeced in a fake ticket scam and all fingers were suddenly pointing at Morris. Cash was unaccounted for, and there were bank accounts in Morris's name into which huge sums had appeared, and from which they had then swiftly disappeared. How were people meant to react when the man they had trusted – had loved – was revealed to be a common thief?

"You know I have always fought his corner," she said.

Newton frowned. "You still think he's innocent. That alibi of his..."

"He mentions it in his letter." She took out the letter. Still unopened in her bag was the more official one, addressed to PD Bakewell. *That* would have to be dealt with at another time.

She unfolded Morris's letter. "He's provided more details about the café he was in at the time he was allegedly withdrawing funds from the Hackney Mutual Bank."

Newton shook his head. He didn't want to hear about it.

"He also mentions," she said, watching Newton carefully, "that he's heard – Lord knows how – that Chartwell and Crouch is selling off some of its assets. Which, as I think we both know, means the buses."

Newton placed a teapot and two mugs on the table, pretending not to hear.

"Were you perhaps thinking that by removing the engines, you could prevent the sale?" Diana asked.

"Well, it's not *just* that," he said. "The maintenance schedule suggests that it's about time they were done. Although it would be unfortunate if their absence prevented any test drives, I suppose."

Newton's attempt to look guileless was not successful.

"Oh Newton," she said, "this must be really tough for you. But don't you think that the sort of person who might buy these buses is unlikely to be deterred by such a thing? In fact, they might even be encouraged that the maintenance schedule is so very thorough."

"What else can I do, though?"

"You'll do what you always do and make sure the buses are well cared for," said Diana. "As for fixing the wider problems at Chartwell and Crouch, I think that's beyond you, me or any of us."

And suddenly Newton, a man who often seemed to have the emotional range of a robot, burst into tears. He sagged into a chair, shoulders shaking, and just cried.

"I can't... I can't..."

Diana reached out a hand to him but Gus was there first. The cat bounced onto the table, meowing in concern, and headbutted the weeping bus driver.

"Don't, Gus," he mumbled. "You'll get grease on you."

Gus ignored him, continuing to headbutt. His gaze blank, Newton plunged his hand into the cat's fur. Diana watched, knowing the cat's companionship was better than anything she could offer.

CHAPTER FIVE

ZAF and his new classmates spent much of the day on a tour of the Guild building. It was surprisingly well-maintained and comfortable. They stopped at the canteen for lunch.

The food was fine, but it was a canteen of the old school with only one hot option each day. Today it was shepherd's pie, or salad, or a jacket potato. The jacket potatoes were wrinkled, the skins looking like they could break teeth.

Zaf opted for the shepherd's pie and asked for extra grated cheese to be sprinkled on top.

The canteen was almost full. There was a mixture of people: Guild staff, businesspeople, and a few worn-looking men who might have just come in off the streets.

"The canteen is also for the people using the hostel next door," Parvani told them. "Both Guild students and some homeless people."

Zaf listened out for judgement in her words, but couldn't hear any.

"We women students get our own floor," she said. She met his eye. "I can't afford London rent prices at the moment."

Despite the Hogwarts air of the building, Zaf saw modern ovens and dishwashers in the kitchen. It was a similar story in the fitness centre which they visited after lunch. There was lots of up-to-date exercise equipment.

"We going to have a session on the free weights?" Jed whispered to Zaf.

Zaf smiled. He was built for speed and grace, especially for throwing shapes on the dance floor. Jed was of a similar build, although it was always possible he was hiding a buff physique under that shirt.

"There will be a physical side to your training," explained Carolyn as they walked through the gym. "We try to be inclusive of all levels of physical ability, but in our profession it's important to be aware of your entire group's mobility needs, so we will exercise together. Bring something comfortable with you, as there will be a daily jog. Nothing you won't all be able to manage."

"Jog?" coughed Jed.

Zaf noticed that pumped-up Josephine looked thrilled at the idea.

The tour concluded with a walk around the area of St Paul's. Bounded on two sides by busy roads and on the other sides by financial buildings, the area around the Cathedral was like a small village of carefully tended gardens, populated with shops, benches and lots of space to relax around Paternoster Square.

The day was soon over, and Zaf was trying to wrap his head around the timetable and all the different locations, as well as everybody's names.

As they left he spotted Diana approach, waving.

"I see your mum's come to collect you at the school gate," said Jed.

Zaf groaned and looked about to see if Ariadne had come too.

Jed gave a mock sad sniff. "And I see mine isn't here. Sometimes I don't think she's my real mum at all..."

His silly sad face broke into a grin. He slapped Zaf on the back, did a finger-pistol-shooting farewell to Parvani and headed off. Zaf said goodbye to Parvani and went over to Diana.

"Are you seriously going to be dropping me off and picking me up every day?" he said.

Diana gave him a quizzical look. "Oh, I'm not here for you. I'm dropping in on Carolyn."

"To see how my first day went."

"Because she's an old friend," Diana insisted. "Things to catch up on. I'm sure I'll catch up with you later."

CHAPTER SIX

Carolyn Desanti's office at the Guild of Tourism looked more like a Victorian scholar's study or even a galleon captain's staterooms than an office, its dark wooden shelves rammed with books and papers.

Carolyn's chair behind the polished desk was an over-stuffed leather thing that creaked as she moved from it. There were two similar chairs by the occasional table at the window. The window, the focal point of the room, was a tall arch which looked directly across St Paul's churchyard at the massive dome of the Cathedral.

From a certain point, possibly low down on the carpeted floor, Diana suspected, the lead-covered dome of the Cathedral and the arch of the window might line up almost perfectly.

Carolyn gave Diana a tired look and gestured to the silver tray on the occasional table.

"I've had the kitchen staff send up tea, but I suspect I'm in need of something stronger."

She opened a Tantalus cabinet by the wall and pulled out a bottle of sherry.

Diana took a seat by the window.

"Drinking at the office?"

"The sun is well past the yardarm," Carolyn replied. "And this feels more like my home than an office sometimes."

Diana smiled. "I rarely associate you with this place, you know. When I picture Carolyn Desanti, I see a woman up to her ankles in mud, the wind whipping off the Thames, sifting through bones and pottery and other gems on the banks of the river."

Carolyn's sigh was wistful. "Mudlarking gets the media attention, but it hardly pays the bills. A messy divorce and poor book sales do rather force one to re-evaluate the boring but necessary things in life."

She picked up two sherry glasses. Diana nodded.

"College life doesn't suit you?" Diana asked.

"An administrative nightmare. Oh, Sam Blackthorn is a fine lecturer. He's got a voice that could give Sir David Attenborough a run for his money. He's enthralling and knowledgeable and has turned out quality tour guides for over twenty years."

"I recall." Diana had gained her own certification under Dr Blackthorn.

Carolyn passed her a small sherry schooner filled nearly to the brim.

"Thank you," said Diana.

"But Sam is a teacher, not an administrator. He comes across as a ringmaster, but he's of no use when it comes to mucking out the elephants."

"Curious metaphor."

"Oh." Carolyn plonked into the chair beside Diana. "My mind is mush at this time of day."

She held her glass out and Diana chinked it with hers.

Outside, the setting sun painted the walls of St Paul's Cathedral a rosy pink.

"We've got Georg Strandman starting with us again tomorrow," Carolyn said. "You know him?"

Diana, who prided herself on remembering almost everyone she had ever met, shook her head.

"Estonian by birth. Taught here decades ago," Carolyn continued. "Apparently, a true academic. But has spent the last ten years plus doing church work in Egypt. A fine addition, by all accounts." She looked sideways at her desk. "But I suspect he won't be lending a hand when it comes to budgetary or personnel matters."

Carolyn paused, to sup half her glass in a single draft. She slapped the arm of her chair. "And how are things with our finest alumna?"

Diana gave her a wry look. "Finest alumna? Me? Can I get that on tape?"

"So that you could share it with a certain Ariadne Webb?"

Diana laughed.

"You two were the best of friends once," Carolyn reminded her.

"A lot of water under the bridge since then," Diana replied. "The music business. Friendships ruined. Ariadne and Pascal – you remember Pascal? Music producer turned restaurant critic? – his battles with booze, their split, and then our mutual friend, Morris..."

"Nasty business."

"Actually, I received a letter today."

Diana went to her bag and pulled out the two letters she'd received that morning. She'd had every intention of discussing the letter from Morris, but surprised herself by putting that one back and bringing out the letter addressed to PD Bakewell instead.

"*Actually*, I had this most peculiar and threatening letter this morning."

"Threatening?" Carolyn sat up in her chair.

"See what you make of it."

Diana passed it over.

"Who's PD Bakewell?" Carolyn.

"Ah, that's the nub of the matter. PD Bakewell is me."

Curious, Carolyn downed the rest of her sherry and opened the letter.

"A letter from Shivdler Legal, representing one Kamran Dadashov."

"The rich guy who owns the house I live in. My landlord, in effect."

"I thought that dark and brooding chap was your landlord."

"That's Alexsei, his son. Nice boy, a bit of a dilettante, but he's always been fair to me."

Carolyn read the rest of the letter in silence. Diana refilled Carolyn's glass. She'd barely touched her own.

Carolyn's eyebrows rose as she read.

"So," she said at last, "you had a long-standing and very favourable rent agreement with the house's previous owner, Mr G Harrison. That wasn't...?"

Diana nodded. "A certain Mr George Harrison, of Beatles fame. He owned the house in the seventies. He rented out spaces to musicians of all sorts. And it was what you'd call a peppercorn rent agreement, one which the Dadashovs agreed to honour when they bought the place. That flat? In Pimlico? On my tour guide salary? I've been lucky to get away with paying such low rent for so many years."

"But the gist of this letter is that your signature on the rent agreement is Diana Bakewell and – have I got this right? – you're not Diana Bakewell."

Diana wafted her hand over herself. "Meet *Patricia* Diana Bakewell. I never liked my given name, and for as long as I can remember even my parents called me Diana."

"So, these Shivdler Legal people are saying that since you signed the agreement with the wrong name, the agreement is null and void and they're going to evict you?"

"Ah." None of it had seemed real to Diana until that point. The threats from the law firm seemed like so much hot air and bluster, to be taken no more seriously more than a badly worded scam e-mail. "I think that's very much what it is saying."

"Can they do that?"

"I believe they are already doing it. There's an eviction date on the letter."

Carolyn was stunned. "Why aren't you screaming with rage? Why aren't you throwing your arms up in the air and yelling 'I'm mad as hell and I'm not going to take it any more'?"

"Let me get over the shock, and I probably will," she said.

Diana realised now that her hand holding the sherry was trembling. She drank it down to stop the liquid slopping around, and then she realised she could do with another.

"I don't suppose an old girl of the Guild of Tourism could get a few million quid to assist with legal fees?" she joked.

Carolyn poured her another glass, holding her hand to steady it.

"Life throws strange and terrible problems at us," she said. "Sometime radical solutions are called for."

"Oh, I'm prepared to get radical."

Diana stayed far longer than she had intended, and they both drank far more than they probably ought to have drunk. It had gone nine o'clock and the sky was almost completely dark by the time Diana left.

"Push comes to shove, there's always a room at the hostel next door," said Carolyn as she saw Diana out of the college's main door.

"Let's hope it doesn't come to that." Diana moved off across the churchyard, the warmth of companionship and the chill of her predicament vying for space inside her head.

There were lights on in the hostel next door. A shadow moved.

Diana looked up. A fat and grizzled man with a dirty, heavily stained coat and an orange bobble hat stood on a first floor corridor, hands against the floor to ceiling window. He was looking out with something like a pained expression on his face. His gaze dropped and he saw Diana. She must have been little more than a shadow in the orange streetlight to him, but his eyes widened as if he'd seen a ghost, and he pushed himself away from the window and disappeared.

Diana dwelt on it for only a moment. Clearly the dirty man had been upset by something. They all had their own problems. But it was like she'd said to Zaf. Life was often difficult, but it wasn't as though anyone had died.

CHAPTER SEVEN

Zaf arrived early at St Paul's tube station. He'd woken early and decided that much as he loved Diana, he wasn't going to be accompanied to school by his mum again, so he was up, out and three miles across London with at least an hour to spare before lessons were due to begin.

Coming through the gates from Paternoster Square, he was nearly run into by a man staggering out of the entrance to the nearby hostel with a mobile phone in his hand.

"Hey, bud!" said Zaf, warning him off. He spotted the panic in the man's eyes and the tremor in his hands. "What is it? You OK?"

The man focussed on him. "Sorry, sorry. ... need ambulance."

"What?"

"Damned phone. I can't..." He turned to look up at the hostel building. "I need an ambulance. He's not breathing."

"Who? Show me."

Zaf wasn't a man of action. He was a lover, an artist, a dancer. But when he was faced with an emergency, especially someone else's emergency, he could move quickly.

"Show me," he repeated. "Here." He took the man's phone, dialled 999 and passed it back to him.

The man led Zaf into the hostel. This part of the building was definitely the medieval alms house Diana had spoken of. But almost immediately, they were moving through a side door into a twentieth century building. The large reception area had white tiling and formal lime green seating.

"Dead. I think he's dead," the man ahead of Zaf was saying into his phone. "Arpinder. Reception morning shift. I just got in a couple of hours ago."

Arpinder waved Zaf up the stairs. "First floor. Third room along. No, second."

Zaf bounded ahead. He had some first aid training, but little beyond recovery positions and chest compressions.

He pushed through a swing door. The corridor was at the front of the building, tall windows to one side, a series of closed doors on the other. Partway down the corridor, a sheet of plastic had been taped in place to seal off that part of the building, matching the scaffolding on the outside of the building.

A nearby room door was open. Zaf peered inside. The room wasn't large. There was a cupboard, a desk-cum-dressing table, a wardrobe, and a single bed. A fat grey-haired man lay on the bed, fully dressed with stained trousers, a faded T-shirt and an orange knitted hat as though the room was too cold.

His eyes were open and staring upwards. Not a good sign.

"Hey, there," said Zaf, his voice cracking. "I'm Zaf. I'm just going to check you."

He put his hand on the man's wrist. It was cold. Not ice cold, not fridge cold. Just devoid of heat. And when Zaf tried to lift the arm, it didn't move.

Without thinking, he forced his fingers under the man's wrist, seeking a pulse. There was none.

"Zaf? What are you doing here?"

Fellow student Parvani was at the door beside the receptionist, Arpinder, who was still on the phone.

"He's dead." Zaf felt his mouth fall open.

Arpinder relayed the information to the emergency services.

Parvani dropped her rucksack to the floor in the corridor and squeezed into the room with Zaf. She put her fingers into the folds of the man's neck, vainly seeking a pulse. Zaf watched her. Should she be touching the man?

"He's covered in sweat," she said.

A sweaty musk emanated from the man. His clothes were unclean and twisted untidily around him.

And there was another smell, woody sweet and citrussy. Not an air freshener, but something more vibrant and natural, like a cologne or incense.

"I think he's been dead a while," Zaf said.

Parvani nodded.

Outside, there was the sound of a siren. Either the ambulance had set a record for response time, or time had flown while they'd been dealing with the man.

"I don't know his name," Arpinder was saying. "It'll be on the register."

Inside a wallet on the dresser, beside some drink bottles and a dirty dinner plate, Zaf found a swipe card key. He pulled it out. On the piece of card that came out with it, someone had written the name 'Marek Bogacki'. Zaf said it out loud, trying to find the pronunciation.

He looked at Arpinder. "His name was Marek."

Arpinder nodded.

Zaf and Parvani stepped out of the room into the fresher air and the light of the corridor. Arpinder dashed downstairs to meet the paramedics.

"You noticed the miosis?" said Parvani.

"The what?" asked Zaf.

"His pupils. They were tiny."

Zaf couldn't tell if she was being ghoulish or just had a bizarre fascination with the human body.

A door opened further down the corridor and an older man in a tweed coat and wire-framed glasses backed out of the room, a battered gladstone bag in his hand. Zaf pulled the door shut a little, as if the dead man might need privacy.

The older man saw them and gave a double take. "Everything all right?"

"Oh, um..." said Zaf.

"No," said Parvani. "A man has died in here."

The man's greying eyebrows rose. "Died?" He had an accent. European somewhere.

"Yes. We're just—"

"Yes, of course," said the man. "How sad. Is everything in hand? I have lectures to deliver."

Boots clattered on the stairs. Two green-clad paramedics came onto the corridor and Zaf and Parvani squeezed out of the way to let them through. Arpinder followed; Zaf imagined there was barely room for the three of them in the small bedroom.

"As I say..." began the man from two doors down.

"Are you a lecturer at the Guild of Tourism?" asked Parvani.

He tipped his head in acknowledgement. "I am Georg Strandman. Now, if you'll excuse me."

"Oh, you're our lecturer." Zaf recognised the name.

"Is that so?"

Zaf felt a little like an unhelpful bystander.

"We could show you the way," he Zaf. "You're new, right?"

"Flew in from Egypt, yes?" said Parvani.

It was a relief to talk about something else, anything but the poor dead man in the hostel room.

"Must be a beautiful country," Parvani said.

"It is," Georg agreed.

Outside, Georg started to turn left, then turned again as Zaf pointed the other way. Zaf shuddered, thinking of the body on the bed.

As they steered Georg into the Guild of Tourism, he leaned over to Parvani.

"What's that business about mitosis?"

"Miosis," she said. "The contracting of the pupils."

"Which means what?"

Parvani gave him a serious look. "Drugs. Opioids."

"Oh."

She leaned in, lowering her voice. "Or poison."

CHAPTER EIGHT

Zaf and Parvani dropped Georg off at the Guild reception where he was greeted almost immediately by Dr Blackthorn. They were both big men, both bearded. However, where Dr Blackthorn had a mountain-man physique and a bushy beard to match, Georg was just a late middle-aged man who looked like he'd ditched exercise years before and forgotten to shave for a week or two.

The classroom they were sent to was panelled with golden-coloured wood. It was old-fashioned, but in a reassuring and timeless way, with individual chairs and tables gathered in a horseshoe shape.

Zaf's first instinct was to choose the spot closest to the door, but that was the impatient teenage version of himself that wanted to race off the moment class finished. Where should the keen and professional version of himself sit? Centre back was a focal point of sorts. He'd take the seat next to that one. He didn't need the pressure of being in the limelight from the start.

Jed slid into the seat next to him.

"Tell me everything," he said.

Zaf looked at him. "What?"

"Don't give me that. You found a body. In the hostel."

Zaf frowned. How did he know?

"It's gossip, this is a closed community," Jed said. "Everyone knows. And most of the stuff they 'know' didn't really happen. So spill the beans."

Parvani sat down next to Jed and began laying out stationery from her bag, lining up a neat row of pencils so that they sat at ninety degrees to the pristine notepad. Should Zaf have brought more stationery?

Jed gave him a dig in the ribs and Zaf recounted the events of the morning so far, with Parvani correcting him every time he made a factual error. She was an expert at bleeding all the drama out of an anecdote.

"That's all," he said at last.

Jed nodded. "Wow. You do attract drama."

Zaf opened his mouth to object but then remembered the other bodies he and Diana had found. Maybe Jed had a point.

The other students in their group were filing in, six of them in total. The rest had been put in classes elsewhere. Shortly after all the seats were filled, Carolyn Desanti came in to address the group with Georg in tow.

"Everyone, this is your teacher for today. Georg Strandman. Renowned ecclesiastical historian and, I hear, one of the finest teachers the Guild of Tourism ever had."

Georg mumbled embarrassed thanks and Carolyn left him to it. He looked about, as if unsure where to start, then put his gladstone bag down beside the front lectern.

"I suppose I'm here then," he said. He shrugged off his heavy coat. Underneath he wore a cardigan and a shirt. The buttons of both strained somewhat at his girth.

"Apologies for my lateness on this, my first day here. I hope you can forgive me, as I was caught up with a very unfortunate incident. A man has lost his life, so can we please take a moment to respectfully acknowledge our lost brother, Marek Bogacki."

He bowed his head, hands together. The students followed suit. Zaf thought the powerfully-built woman, Josephine, looked annoyed at the delay to the start of the day.

After a suitable period, Georg raised his head and cast about the room. "I think we will have a few minutes to introduce each other. I am Georg Strandman. I am an ecclesiastical historian as Carolyn has told you. I am Estonian. Anyone else here Estonian? No? Oh. It is a lovely country. OK. Now, you." He pointed a finger at a student at random.

Each student spent a few moments on the perennially awful task of summarising themselves in a couple of bullet points. In every group, there would always be somebody who just couldn't do it, and would launch into a story instead. In this group, Josephine was that person.

"I was part of a rugby coaching academy in the nineties. We took prep school kids and turned them into good solid rugby players. A few casualties on our summer camping trip to the Brecon Beacons that one time. This one lad slipped on some scree and totally degloved his—"

"—Fascinating stuff, Josephine," said Georg, "but how did you end up here at the Guild?"

"I was coming to that," said Josephine. "It turns out that modern parents just don't want to toughen up their kids as per my speciality, but they do still love to educate them. I specialise in setting up tours for schools and clubs. Sporting legends and locations."

"So," said Georg. "Many of you have been recommended

to attend this course by colleagues and friends. What are you looking forward to? What do you think we are going to do?"

Zaf had nothing. He was fairly sure that Diana had never described any specifics. The look on Jed's face suggested that Ariadne hadn't either.

Josephine had a hand in the air. "Yes! Obviously we do the blindfold icebreaker first, but then I heard there was a daily sprint around St Paul's."

There was a subtle exhalation from the rest of the group. It wasn't loud enough to qualify as a groan, but it made Georg raise an eyebrow. "Sprint?"

"Carolyn described it as a jog," Zaf explained.

Georg smiled. "Well, if Josephine chooses to sprint rather than jog, I think we can allow her that. How about it, everybody? Good. A brisk walk for me. A meander, even. That's settled then. And then we'll have the – the icebreaker, was it? Who would care to explain things to the uninitiated?"

Parvani raised her hand. "We all have ten minutes to familiarise ourselves with the interior of St Paul's, and then we must inform an imaginary tour group, while blindfolded. I assumed we'd do that early in the day though, before the Cathedral fills up with people?"

"Good. Well, before we do, I think it would be good to encourage a little competition. This class will have two teams."

"Teams?" said a student.

"It *is* bloody Gryffindor and Slytherin," Jed whispered to Zaf.

"You," said Georg, pointing at Josephine. "And you." He pointed at Parvani. "Pick your teams for the day's challenges."

Zaf was dismayed. This reminded him of one of the worst experiences from his childhood: being selected for PE teams. It was a brutal and humiliating thing. Why were they doing this?

"I choose Sacha," said Josephine, getting in first. She looked pleased with herself as Sacha walked over.

Parvani looked across at the crowd, uneasy with the task she'd been given. "Jed?"

As Jed walked over, Josephine gave a cruel smirk, mocking her choice. It made Zaf hope with all his heart that she wouldn't choose him, and yet he realised that not being chosen brought its own brand of pain, as it meant he would be the very last to be picked.

Josephine made a big show out of choosing between Zaf and Adi, a quiet woman of around Zaf's age. She looked them up and down as if checking for obvious defects. "Adi," she sighed eventually, as if it pained her to select either of the pitiful specimens before her.

Zaf gave a small shrug and trotted over to join Parvani and Jed. "Well that was pretty awful."

"I'm so sorry, Zaf. This looks like a good group to me, though," said Parvani.

"Yeah, high fives," said Jed, holding up a hand to each of them.

They high-fived and smiled at each other, then turned to face the other group.

"Game on," muttered Jed with a wink.

CHAPTER NINE

GEORG HAD BEEN true to his word about his gentle meander. Josephine claimed she could have sprinted round St Paul's Cathedral half a dozen times in the time it took him to complete his circuit.

As they passed the hostel, they couldn't help but look over. The ambulance had gone and now there was a police car on the pavement.

Zaf and Jed walked side by side. "So Parvani thinks it was drugs?" said Jed.

Zaf shrugged. "I don't want to judge, but the guy looked homeless. His clothes were dirty. There was a scuzzy backpack in the corner of the room."

"Lot of homeless people do drugs," Jed said.

"Or she said it might be poison."

"What is she? A forensic pathologist?"

Zaf smiled. She had mentioned being a scientist at Imperial College.

Even at a gentle amble, Georg was catching up with them. Parvani, a tiny dot next to the big guy, was chatting to him.

When the whole group had gathered, they walked over to St Paul's. Josephine pumped the air, red-cheeked.

"Go explore," said Georg, waving his hands at the Cathedral. "See what you can see. I'm going to be putting some of you on the spot in a bit."

Parvani led her team into the Cathedral. Zaf had been here before, both as tour guide and tourist, but the sheer size of the place never failed to impress him. It was a visual feast in every direction. The floor was huge with shiny, black and white checkerboard tiles. Patterned tiles marked out the font and the dome.

"See if you can discern any difference in the sound when you face in different directions," said Parvani. "Count steps between things. What else?"

"We should taste the air, like a snake," said Jed, flicking his tongue out.

Parvani gave him a look. "Right. We should also see if there are any distinctive smells."

As they walked around inside the Cathedral the group paced, counted and memorised.

"Back at the font in ten minutes," called Georg. "Stay on this floor please."

Zaf walked along the floor. Even if he'd been asked to describe the view in front of him with his eyes wide open, there was so much to look at that he was sure he'd miss something out. The walls were lined with pale stone, possibly marble. Carvings, plaques, statues and gilt highlights were everywhere. Even the lighting fixtures were breathtaking. He looked up and found the effort of trying to absorb all the arches and windows almost dizzying. And then, of course, there was the famous dome.

"Time's up," said Jed.

"Really?" Zaf had barely looked at anything beyond first impressions. He wasn't prepared for this.

Jed leaned into him as they all drew back to Georg, like ducklings back to their mother.

"So, why would anyone poison a homeless guy?"

Zaf looked at him. "We're meant to be focussing on the Cathedral."

"It just doesn't make sense."

"If someone is poisoned, it doesn't mean anyone else has done it. I'm sure there are lots of accidental poisonings every year."

"Sounds like some people have plenty to talk about," said Georg, as they gathered at the font. "Zaf, yes? Shall we start with you?"

"Oh no." Zaf tried to shrink back, but felt a shove in the back as Jed pushed him forward. Georg pulled a scarf out of his pocket and blindfolded him.

"I will steer you to a point on the Cathedral floor," Georg said. "You'll be quite safe."

Zaf allowed himself to be guided. He had no idea where he was, or even which direction he was facing. He was vaguely aware that the group had been following along, as he could hear them shuffling.

"Here we are Zaf, you can stand here. Now, would you speak to the group and tell them what you can see?"

Blind to the world, Zaf realised he'd have no choice but to wing it.

"Here we are on the Cathedral floor of St Paul's. Christopher Wren built this spectacular building three hundred years ago, although there have been churches on this site for well over a thousand years. He made it visually stunning. The tiled floor, the marble walls and of course, towering above us, the iconic dome."

He paused to gather his thoughts.

"You all came in through the enormous West Entrance and passed the font. There are baptisms here at St Paul's, as well as weddings."

Zaf removed the blindfold while the group clapped. He was standing next to a door that led away to what was probably the vestry.

Georg came over. "Good solid strategy. Talk about general things. You did well. Join the others."

As Zaf joined the group Georg selected Josephine. She was blindfolded and they all followed as she was led around in an exaggerated figure of eight shape so that she ended up not far away from where Zaf had been, but facing a different direction.

"Well here we are in St Paul's," said Josephine. "I want to point out the dome of course."

There was a cough from someone in the group.

"Which is on my left." Josephine raised a hand and pointed left.

Zaf wondered whether they had agreed a code, so that Josephine could be fed information from her teammates.

"And, of course, the high altar," Josephine said.

There was a sneeze. Now Zaf was sure there was a code. He coughed loudly.

"The high altar. Even though it's out of sight, it's also on the left."

Zaf grinned. He'd given Josephine a bum steer. Jed had spotted what was happening, and gave Zaf a look, eyebrows raised.

The two of them took turns coughing, ensuring cheating

was off the table. Josephine stumbled through, her confidence diminishing by the second.

When she eventually removed the scarf, she looked furious.

CHAPTER TEN

Georg and his students spent the morning in the Cathedral. When they emerged at lunchtime, Dr Blackthorn was waiting outside the Guild building. He was talking to Georg in hushed tones.

Georg nodded and turned to the students. “Zaf, Parvani, with me. The rest of you go inside with the good doctor.”

Zaf followed Georg. Why had they been singled out?

He soon found out. Georg was leading them past the police car, to the hostel.

Two uniformed officers were waiting in the reception. Above and outside, workmen were drilling.

“We just need to get some details down,” one of the officers said, raising his voice over the noise.

“Just a formality, I assume,” Georg replied.

“Unexplained deaths are dealt with by the coroner.”

“But the man, he just had a heart attack, yes?”

The officers exchanged glances and got on with the interviews. Zaf told them everything he knew, from bumping into Arpinder to the paramedics arriving.

The policeman asked Zaf for photo ID. He handed over his card, the one he used for getting into bars. The other officer scrutinised Georg's passport. Georg put it away.

As Zaf was finishing up, one of the officers said, "Miss Kadivar. You said you were at these stairs here when you heard the commotion."

"That's right."

"But if your room was down the far end, wouldn't it have been more obvious for you to come down the far stairs? Over there?"

Parvani looked from the door, to one set of stairs, then to the other.

"It was my first night here," she said. "I'll know better in future."

Georg led Zaf and Parvani outside. He put a hand on each of their shoulders. "I think that is perhaps the end of today's learning. The doctor has sent the rest of the class home."

"Already?" Parvani sounded like she'd been hoping for more time.

"Tomorrow, you start fresh. I wish you a good evening."

Jed was sitting on a low wall nearby. He stood up and went over to them once they'd moved away from Georg. "The rozzers trying to finger you for the murder?"

"It's not a murder," Parvani said.

"They had searching questions for Parvani," Zaf added, teasing.

Jed narrowed his eyes at the retreating figure of Georg. "Interesting character."

"What does that mean?" Zaf said.

"He's got that absent-minded professor thing going on, but there's also a bit of the wayward uncle about him. Still." Jed took a deep breath. "I did learn a lot today."

"Did he actually *teach* us anything?" Parvani said. "I hope we'll be spending our evening prepping for tomorrow."

Zaf saw that her notebook was bristling with stickers and page markers. When had she had time to do that?

"Not me," he said. "I'm off to meet my partner, Alexsei. Early finish means we can meet up."

"He's a lucky boy," Jed said with a curl of his lips. "How long have the two of you been together?"

"We're just coming up to our six month anniversary." Zaf couldn't help grinning. "I'm meeting him for a coffee in Soho to plan how we'll celebrate."

Parvani smiled. "That's so lovely. It's great when you feel as though you've got to the point that you properly know someone."

"I hope I have." Zaf nodded. "He is like the missing pieces of me."

"Wow. Cheesy. Like mountains of cheddar there, mate."

"You've got no missing pieces, Zaf." Parvani was more earnest.

"He grounds me. I can be a bit full-on sometimes but with him I can be quieter. He says a similar thing about me, that I pull him out of his comfort zone. Anyway..."

Zaf hurried off. The Central Line tube from St Paul's took him to Oxford Circus, and five minutes later was standing in line with Alexsei outside a coffee shop in Soho. The queue snaked down the street, but they were happy to wait and drink in the atmosphere.

"Ooh nice, you're wearing the shirt I got you," Zaf said.

Alexsei gave a shrug. "It's now my favourite shirt."

"I still can't believe you never owned anything vintage before. That there is a genuine knock-off Vivienne Westwood pirate shirt."

Alexsei laughed. "I had a privileged upbringing. I could probably get a genuine knock-off Vivienne Westwood made to measure if I wanted."

"Ah, but you probably wouldn't think to do it. The great thing about vintage is that it presents you with an endless palette of possibilities, from every era."

"You know that you have just described yourself don't you? An endless palette of possibilities."

"I'll take that compliment and put in my wallet for a rainy day."

"It's weird. I can do more or less as I please and yet I don't think I even knew what I wanted. You've opened my mind, Zaf."

Zaf grinned. "We make a good team."

"I think so."

"You know, in the spirit of open minds and endless possibilities, for our six month anniversary we should do something we've never done."

"Like what?"

"Not sure. Maybe go and learn something new like Spanish or welding."

Alexsei looked horrified.

"Or something," Zaf said. "Let's have a think."

"Welding? Seriously?" Alexsei pulled a face. "Although would we have to wear those overalls like the Formula One pit crew?"

Zaf nodded. He had no idea what outfit was appropriate for welding, but the mental image appealed.

"Hunky pit mechanic." He put a hand on Alexsei's chest.

"Or maybe just knock-off pirate for today." The queue moved, and they were one step closer to the coffee shop.

"So, how was your day at college?" Alexsei said.
Zaf puffed out his cheeks. "Where to begin?"

CHAPTER ELEVEN

DIANA HEARD Zaf enter the sub-divided house in Eccleston Square. She went out to the stairwell and called to him to come up.

"I want to chat to you for a minute."

There were low sounds of conversation between Zaf and Alexsei and then heavy, tired footsteps on the stairs.

"I didn't want to bother you," she said. "I'm sure you've had an eventful day."

"You wouldn't believe how eventful." He turned the corner of the stairs. "I must share some things with you. Maybe you can make sense of them."

"Oh?"

She had prepared herself for an important chat, the sharing of the information from the law firm's letter. But this sounded interesting.

"A man died today."

"What?" Diana hurried him into her flat.

Diana had occupied the first floor of the house for many years. It was filled with items of furnishing and decoration that, if not directly reflecting her personality, at least created a space where she could feel at home. She had put out the things for tea on the trunk coffee table she'd picked up in a Portobello shop and had laid out a selection of biscuits.

"A man at the hostel next to the college," Zaf said. "An unexplained death."

"So, not at the Guild? Nothing you saw?"

"Oh, no. The receptionist was outside, flapping about in panic and – I didn't do anything really – but I went inside. Did basic first aid while the receptionist, Arpinder, called the emergency services."

"Oh, my goodness." Diana gave his arm a comforting squeeze. "That must have been horrible. I know you've seen bodies before—"

"I don't make a hobby of it."

"No, of course."

Zaf sat down and picked up a chocolate biscuit. "The thing I can't get out of my mind was the smell."

"Of the man?"

"No. Well, yes. He was... No, it was this other smell." Zaf's brow was creased into tight lines. "This smell. Like a perfume smell. A woodsmoke and fruit type smell. I guess it stuck in my mind because he... I guess he was a homeless guy. Marek something. Polish, I think." Zaf gestured with his arms, as if he were trying to drag Diana into the scene with him. "He was filthy and had been sleeping in all his clothes, even this little orange bobble hat."

"Orange?"

Diana was struck by a recollection from the night before. When she'd come out of the Guild, having said goodbye to Carolyn, she'd seen that man with the orange knitted hat. He'd been standing in the window of the hostel, visible from the pavement outside. She recalled the look of anguish on his face and then the horrified surprise at seeing her in the dark churchyard outside.

"I saw him."

"You what?" Zaf said. "You saw who?"

"Big feller, yes? Unshaven."

"That's him," she said.

"And the orange hat. Last night. I'd been to see Carolyn and..." She put her hand on his arm again. "Life is fleeting."

"Death is a lot to process."

He ate another biscuit. It was perhaps his third.

"You'll ruin your dinner," she said.

He picked up a cup of tea. "You said you had something you wanted to discuss with me."

Diana considered telling him it wasn't as important as a man's death but in truth, to her, to both of them, it almost certainly was.

"This letter." She put the letter from Shivdler Legal to one PD Bakewell on the table.

"Oh. I had wondered who that was for."

"Just read it."

"Have you been crying?"

"Just read it." Propelled by an impetus to do something, anything, she stood up and paced the room.

"An *irregularity* in your rent agreement?" Zaf said as he read. His hands were shaking by the time he'd finished. "Have I read this right?"

She nodded. "My name. They're saying there's an 'irregularity', as they call it, and that my tenancy agreement is therefore void."

"Can you renegotiate?"

"They've given an eviction date." She pointed at the letter.

Zaf looked at it. "That's within the week. They can't."

"They can. Apparently. I think they can."

He whirled around, taking in the flat – her home, their home – for the first time.

"It's so unfair. What does Alexsei say about it?"

Diana looked out through the window, across the gardens, a view she was soon to lose. "I'm not even sure Alexsei knows. I haven't spoken to him about it."

Zaf went to the door. "I'll speak to him. He can speak to these legal people. He can speak to his dad."

"Zaf," Diana said. "Kamran Dadashov has instructed Shivdler to do this. It's a business decision that he has made. I can't imagine him un-making it."

"You're acting like it's already happened. There must be something we can do."

She drew in a breath. "Promise me you won't do anything rash."

"Rash? Oh, you'll see rash all right."

He strode out and stomped downstairs.

CHAPTER TWELVE

Zaf squared his shoulders and knocked at Alexsei's door. The door would be unlocked, and Zaf had a key anyway, but if ever there was a time for knocking, this was it.

Alexsei answered and frowned. "Yes? It was open."

Zaf stood in the doorway, slightly numb. Now it was time to have the conversation, he didn't really know how to begin. "Diana's being evicted. How could you let this happen?"

"Oh man." Alexsei sagged.

"You knew?"

"I suspected." Alexsei sighed. "I had seen some paperwork. I didn't know they would go through with it. Come in, yeah? Let's talk."

"I want to talk here." This was not just a time for knocking, but also for firm stances. "This is the worst thing I've ever heard. Who does that? Who evicts someone from a place that is supposed to be theirs in perpetuity just because they found a stinking *loophole*?"

Alexsei looked away, sheepish. "Businessmen."

"Sorry, what?"

"Businessmen. They are the ones that do things like that. Same as they are the ones who will send an Uber with a birthday gift if they forgot. I cannot fix the way my father is."

"So this is your dad's doing?"

"His hand is in everything."

"He's making Diana homeless. He's met her. They've spent time together. He's going to stab her in the back, just like that."

Alexsei shook his head. For a moment Zaf thought Alexsei meant that Kamran Dadashov hadn't instructed his lawyers to evict Diana. But he was shaking his head at Zaf's misunderstanding.

"Rich people. One of the reasons some of them are rich is that they can separate the business and social parts of their lives completely, even if that separation runs straight through a human being. My father has carried out an aggressive takeover of a man's business one day and then gone to the same man's wedding the next. For them, it really is a case of 'business is business'."

"He's making Diana homeless."

"She has family. Her mother in Bow. She will land on her feet."

"Yes. Yes of course your father would know that. He's even been to her mother's flat, where she made him sandwiches and treated him like a regular person."

"He is not a regular man. And I do not control him."

Zaf shook himself, like a fresh awakening after a cold shower.

"No. Diana is your friend."

"A tenant."

"A friend. And me, I'm... I thought you would be able to stand up to your father."

"This is not my doing."

"No. You've clearly – *carefully* – played no part in this."

Alexsei reached out to take Zaf's hand. "Whatever happens, there will be a place for you. You could move in here with me."

Zaf snatched his hand away. In his pocket, his phone buzzed. "I won't be moving in here, Alexsei." He stepped back from the door.

"What are you doing?" asked Alexsei.

Zaf sniffed and raised his chin. "I think Diana needs me for the time being. Good night, Alexsei."

He turned and forced himself to walk up the stairs, ignoring Alexsei as he stood in the doorway calling his name. As he climbed the flight of stairs to Diana's flat, he pulled out his phone.

Number withheld.

"Yes?"

"Hello," said a male voice. "This is Sergeant McIlkenny from Holborn police station. Can I speak to a, er, Zaf Williams."

"This is he."

"Oh, right. Yes. Well, I just wanted to thank you, Mr Williams, for all your help this morning with the deceased gentlemen at St Paul's."

"Err... no problem."

"I thought you'd like to know that we've had an initial report back from the pathologist, and it appears we're looking at a case of poisoning."

Zaf hesitated. "I see."

"The pathologist thinks the victim had been dead for at least fourteen hours by the time you found him this morning."

"He was very stiff." Zaf continued walking, entering the

flat. He walked into the kitchen, where Diana was reading with a cup of tea in her hand. "Police," he mouthed.

"I'm calling everyone who was in contact with the deceased," Sergeant McIlkenny continued. "If you experience any symptoms—"

Zaf put a hand up to his face. "Is this like that Salisbury poisoning thing? One touch and I'm—"

"It's not a nerve agent, sir. It's not radioactive. It's just bad chemicals. I've been asked to tell you to look out for symptoms including muscle spasms, weakness, excessive sweating..."

Zaf bit his lip. Diana was looking at him, curious.

"Sir, if you experience any of these symptoms, you should go straight to hospital."

"I will."

"Thank you, sir. Good night."

Zaf ended the call and stared at Diana.

"What is it?" she said.

"The homeless man. They're looking at poisoning."

"The homeless man."

Zaf nodded. "They're concerned the rest of us might be contaminated."

"Is that likely?"

Zaf shook his head. "Apparently, when I attended to him, he'd been dead for fourteen hours. We were far too late."

Diana frowned. "What time was that?"

"What time was what? Oh, I dunno. About eight thirty this morning."

Diana's mouth moved, calculating. "That can't be possible."

"At least fourteen hours, the sergeant said."

She shook her head. "I saw him. I told you I saw him, last

night. And I remember looking at the clock above the guild-house door. It had just gone nine, and I saw him in the corridor upstairs. That's little less than twelve hours."

CHAPTER THIRTEEN

Diana's phone rang a few minutes after nine.

"Am I speaking to P D Bakewell?"

"Yes you are." She knew immediately that this was someone from Shivdler. Who else would use a name that she had abandoned years ago? "Who's calling?"

"This is Simeon De Montford from Shivdler Legal. You have of course received a letter from our offices." It was a statement, not a question. "I shall be making a brief visit at your convenience in the next day or two."

"I see." Diana didn't see. "What is the purpose of the visit? Am I able to put forward my side of things? Perhaps there is something to be —"

Simeon gave a small, embarrassed laugh. "Oh no. There is no question of you challenging the outcome. The visit is merely part of our process. It is to ensure that a smooth transition takes place. It's something we've found can be beneficial for all parties. Setting expectations, if you will."

Diana had come across people like Simeon De Montford before. He was sneering at her, with his Oxbridge accent and lawyerly smugness. No part of this was for her benefit. He just wanted to make sure she was going to leave on time.

"Fine. It will need to be early, though. I'll be out at work otherwise."

If she had to accommodate the intrusion, it would be on her terms.

Diana decided to make productive use of the rest of her week.

She knew enough solicitors in the London area, and had phoned a couple with her tenancy agreement issue. The first had suggested the eviction could be challenged on the grounds of Diana's long term residency in the property. The second had argued that the cost of fighting it might outweigh the benefit of winning the argument. The third had laughed, not unkindly, and suggested that Diana's own rental agreement was flawed at best and appeared to be a messy, nested sub-letting agreement which was almost meaningless without further documentation that Diana had no access to.

She was already considering whether the time left before the eviction was better spent arguing her case or beginning the long process of packing up her home and getting ready to leave. She sent a message to her mum, carefully enquiring if she might come and stay over for a 'few days' later in the month. Beverley Bakewell might have been in her eighties and not particularly tech-savvy, but that didn't stop the woman replying almost immediately with a clear affirmative and indicating in the minimum of words that she knew exactly what was going on.

Diana went into work as normal but, in the absence of any actual tours to conduct this week, searched the storerooms at the rear of the depot for any boxes she could use for packing. Gus the cat decided to help with this process, which meant scrabbling over the mountain of boxes she set aside and sitting in his favourites. Diana felt that, in this regard at least, cats and children were very much alike. Give them a box, a place to hide, and they were happier than with any toy money could buy.

Gus seemed to be struggling to decide which box would make him happiest. The big grey tabby cat would settle in one brown cardboard box then immediately scrabble his way out to seek another.

"What are you doing here?" said Newton, ambling over with his morning brew in his hand.

"Finding decent packing boxes."

"Oh, hells. What other things are they selling off from here?"

"Not Chartwell and Crouch. Me. I'm moving out."

"What? From your swanky Pimlico pad?"

"Sometimes there are things you have to do. Even when you don't want to."

There was a furious thumping and scratching from the box next to Diana and then Gus, fur on end like a creature possessed, leapt out, skittering in circles for a minute before diving head first into a new box.

"Your friend is not being overly helpful," Diana told Newton.

"My 'friend' and I are not talking at the moment," he sniffed.

"Really?"

"As far as I'm concerned, he's a traitor to the cause."

"The cause?"

Newton went to the box Gus was currently in, closed up the folding flaps and carried the box ten feet away to another spot in the depot.

"Betrayed me, he has." He took out his phone. "All three buses have been listed for sale."

The Chiltern Street Chartwell and Crouch depot had a 'fleet' of buses, numbering three in total. One was open top, the other two covered. All three were functioning and well-maintained examples of the old red double-decker Routemaster bus. Though there were many red double-decker buses in service around the capital, none held the romanticism or matched the iconic image quite like mid-twentieth century Routemasters.

As Chartwell and Crouch's fortunes continued to crumble, the decision had been made to sell off the buses. This struck Diana as unbelievably short-sighted, given that these buses were the bread and butter of the company. It was like a baker selling their oven or a library selling off their books.

"How is the buses being for sale Gus's fault?" said Diana.

"Look." He held up his phone. The buses were listed for sale, looking their gleaming best in a series of interior and exterior photos.

Diana squinted, unsure what he was on about. Then she saw it.

In every shot, prim and as photogenic as ever, was Gus. That cat loved a camera. Gus sitting on the bonnet on a bus. Gus sitting in the driver's seat, paws on the wheel as though he was driving it. Gus patrolling the upper deck in an image of the original wooden floors.

"Oh. Hardly deliberate."

"He's practically selling them all by himself," Newton argued.

"Still. He's just sharing his love for the buses."

The box Gus sat in rocked as he prowled and played.

"What exactly is all this?" said Paul Kensington, the depot manager, approaching from his tiny office.

"All this?" said Diana.

Paul was wearing his regular short-sleeved shirt and a clip-on tie, giving him the appearance of a schoolboy dressed by his mum. He flung an imperious hand towards the boxes Diana had brought out of storage.

"Doing some tidying up," said Diana.

"Have you no tours to lead?" asked Paul. He knew full well she did not.

She eyed him. "I was going to take a walk over to St John's Wood and do more work on that Beatles walking tour idea."

Paul pursed his lips and nodded. If Chartwell and Crouch was truly going to lose its buses, then Diana had best throw herself into ramping up their better walking tours and devising new ones.

"Well, then you'd best get to it." He marched away.

Diana and Newton exchanged glances.

"Best get on then." She'd found at least six large boxes she could use to pack up her belongings. "And best put these out of the way."

With Gus safely ensconced in one of the boxes, she moved the five others into a neat row along the box wall. As she picked up the fifth empty box, the weight inside shifted and there was a high-pitched 'rawr' of surprise. Gus burst through the closed flaps, clambered onto her shoulders and leapt away.

Surprised, she looked at Newton. "I thought he was in the other one. How does he do it?"

"He's a magician." Newton smiled. "But these boxes do all look the same..."

CHAPTER FOURTEEN

Zaf's morning had been a pair of lectures, one delivered by Carolyn de Santi and the other by Georg Strandman, on the subject of famous London landmarks and locations. It had felt like the equivalent of taxi drivers learning the 'knowledge' of the city. And it was the sort of thing Zaf excelled at. Many months of tour guiding for Chartwell and Crouch had given him a comprehensive knowledge of London's key tourist spots.

Jed Skirmish, with even more months of work at ACE Tours under his belt, felt he was the superior tour guide.

Carolyn's lesson had focused on the more obvious London landmarks. Zaf and Jed had competed to offer the most obscure facts about the Palace of Westminster.

"The Palace has a gymnasium and rifle-shooting range for the use of Members of Parliament," said Jed.

"There's a colony of bees housed on the roof of the Palace, to aid pollination in the local area," said Zaf.

"During World War II, the Crown Jewels were hidden there!"

"The Palace once had a pneumatic railway for mail transportation between buildings!"

By contrast, Georg's session, informal as always, had focused on a different sort of London. His tour guide questioning had centred on the criminal activity associated with London's East End. Zaf tried to compete with Jed's knowledge once more.

"The Kray twins knew Judy Garland and Frank Sinatra," said Jed.

"The Krays managed a West End nightclub and attempted to break into the music industry," said Zaf.

"In the nineteenth century, 'resurrection men' dug up bodies and sold them to doctors!"

"Highwayman Dick Turpin was rumoured to have operated in the East End and carried out robberies there!"

"Rumoured?" said Georg, peering over his wire-framed glasses.

Georg's light questioning of Zaf's fact seemed to put a seal on things. Jed had won that round.

At lunchtime, Zaf sat with Jed and Parvani in the Guild of Tourism canteen. Today's singular meal of choice was 'fish bake'. There was little indication of what the fish was or what it had been baked in, and it was a challenge to work out either.

"You two competing against each other was annoying," said Parvani.

"Because we knew more than you?" said Jed.

Her hesitation told them this was partly true.

"No one could get a work in edgeways with two alpha males competing for dominance."

Zaf laughed and Jed did too. Jed gripped Zaf's slim arm. "Look at us. Do we look like alpha males?"

Zaf pointed a finger at Jed's boyishly beautiful face. "I

suspect this guy spent as much time running away from homophobic alpha males as I did, back in the day."

"Back in the day?" said Jed. "Try every time I go back to my home town."

"Whatever," said Parvani. "With you two going on and on... Did you not see the look on Josephine's face?"

"Was it like a bulldog chewing a nettle?" suggested Jed.

Parvani was unamused. "Seriously, Josephine really has it in for us now."

"She's had it in for everyone from the start," said Jed. "Our best bet is to take the wind out of her sails when we can, and otherwise ignore her."

Parvani shook her head. "How can we ignore her? Did you know that she spent last summer eating a Ford Fiesta?"

Zaf and Jed stopped eating and stared.

"It sounded like...it sounded like you just said Josephine she ate a car," said Zaf.

"She did. She ate a whole car. Don't ask me how or why, but she did. She is obsessed with proving that she's the strongest and the toughest and the best. Look her up."

Jed's fingers flew across his phone. "She really did. Look at these pictures!"

Zaf leaned across and saw that there were two images. In the 'before' picture, Josephine posed with a car, wielding a knife and fork. In the second, 'after' picture, the car was gone.

"She could have just parked it round the corner," joked Zaf. But they both knew she hadn't. Somehow, she'd eaten the whole thing.

"Speaking of things possibly eaten," said Parvani, her tone much quieter and more sombre. "You've not noticed any symptoms, Zaf?"

"Symptoms?" he said and then realised what she meant.

"This that oregano poisoning thing?" said Jed.

"Organophosphate," said Parvani. "You know that's the family of poisons the Russian spies used in their attacks back in twenty-eighteen?"

Zaf felt his skin prickle. Sergeant McIlkenny had assured him it wasn't the nerve agent used in the Salisbury poisonings. But the connection had stayed with him.

"You don't think this Marek Bogacki character was a Russian spy, do you?" whispered Jed.

"The target that time was a defector," said Zaf.

"Whatever."

"And besides, Bogacki is a Polish name, not Russian," said Parvani.

"Spies have aliases," Jed pointed out. "And who can tell the difference between a Polish accent and a Russian one?"

"Poles and Russians can, I'd have thought," Zaf replied.

"Still," said Jed, giving them both meaningful looks, "the police are back at the hostel next door. This thing is not just a simple poisoning, is it?"

CHAPTER FIFTEEN

Diana answered the door. "Mr De Montford."

"Miss Bakewell." The man in the suit, Simeon De Montford, looked exactly as she'd pictured. A little younger than she'd imagined, perhaps, probably under forty, but he had the prim old-fashioned look of a cog in a formidable legal machine.

"Will this take long?" she asked.

"Not at all. I'll just need to take a look in each of the rooms."

She stepped aside with a sigh. There was no point in arguing.

He followed her through her rooms. Part of her wanted to excuse the mess caused by her packing, but she bit down on the urge.

"You have made plans for the move, I trust?" he asked. "You do seem to have rather a lot of possessions."

She stared at him. "Not that it's any of your business."

He raised an eyebrow.

"I know why you're here," she said. "To check that I'm not damaging the place. To make sure I'll be leaving."

He didn't reply.

"So what are you doing to help? Will Dadashov be paying for a removal firm?"

"Mr Dadashov has no obligation to—"

"No. I had hoped I might appeal to him as a fellow human. You can tell him I won't forget what he's done to me."

She closed the door firmly after De Montford left, keen to reinforce the message that the flat was still her home, even if only for a day or two. She needed to take her mind off things. A trip to the hostel would do the trick.

She went to the site to walk through in her mind what she'd seen that night after visiting Carolyn. Reconsidering her plan, she approached the modern hostel building. If she'd really seen what she thought she had, the police officers would need to know.

A policeman in a hi-vis jacket held up a hand. "Sorry, madam. You can't come in here."

"I just wanted to talk to someone."

"You're a journalist?"

Carolyn called out Diana's name from behind him. "Thought it sounded like you." She pushed past the policeman. "She's with me."

"I wanted to speak to the officer in charge." Diana followed Carolyn into the lobby, which was full of policemen.

DS Quigley was standing by the front desk, talking to a young man. Diana had met Quigley before, always in connection with unexplained deaths.

"No, but it's because of the renovation works," the receptionist was saying. "We're giving out a limited number of rooms and recording them here." He spun an untidy ledger around on the counter. "We sign them in and give them a key. I do morning duty." Diana peered at the page, on which the names *G Strandman, M Bogacki* and *J Swann* were scrawled.

Quigley turned to the nearest uniformed officer. "Do we have a statement off these two?"

"The J Swann character departed that morning before the body was found. And Mr Strandman—"

"Is here." A broad, bespectacled man. "And wondering if I can possibly get to my room."

Carolyn stepped close to Diana's ear. "As you can see, it's all go round here. A man has died."

"So I hear."

"You'll be able to return to your room once the forensics team are done," Quigley told the man. "We have been through this."

"Georg," said Carolyn. "I will call you when you can access your room. Don't you have lectures today?"

"Possibly." He had a strong European accent. Estonian, he'd said.

"I've adjusted the timetable for the rest of the week," Carolyn told him. "You're doing the group roleplay exercises and Dr Blackthorn is doing the St Paul's tours."

"This is fine." With that, he left them.

Carolyn squeezed Diana's hand. "This intrusion is making everything worse. The hostel maintenance work has already closed off half the rooms. I know the Clerkenwell Hostel on Farringdon Road is over capacity. The effect on rough sleepers who—"

Quigley turned from the desk. "Ah, the great Diana Bakewell. What are you doing here? Not come to offer your insights into police business again, have you?"

Diana bristled. "Carolyn is a friend of mine."

Quigley looked past Carolyn, into the lobby.

"I think I saw the poisoning victim shortly before he died," Diana continued.

Both Quigley and Carolyn looked at her, eyebrows raised.

"It was the night before he died. I had been visiting you at the Guild. I left at nine and then, out there" – she pointed to the St Paul's churchyard just beyond the partially frosted windows – "I looked up and saw the man, Bogacki, on the floor above."

"You saw Marek Bogacki?" Quigley said.

"I did. He looked alarmed. Maybe distressed. But I saw him, and then he went off."

DS Quigley was noting this down in a pad. "And you know Bogacki? You recognised him?"

"No. Never met him before."

Quigley frowned. "You recognised him?"

"The person I saw matched the description I was given. The orange hat. There aren't many of them about."

"Describe the man you saw for me, please."

Diana searched her memory. "Overweight. Grey-haired, I think. It was at a little distance. The orange knitted hat, obviously."

Quigley nodded. "And this was nine p.m.?"

"I remember looking at the clock next door. Nine p.m."

"Thank you. That's actually useful."

"The time of death was supposedly recorded as at least a couple of hours earlier than that and—"

"No, that's fine." Quigley closed her notebook. "Your information is appreciated."

"If the coroner has said—"

"Greater minds than yours or mine will take a look at all the information. They'll work out what's what."

DCI Sugarbrook had always been the senior officer on the

cases Diana had helped with. "Is Detective Chief Inspector Sugarbrook working this case with you?"

Quigley raised an eyebrow. "Case, Ms Bakewell? A man has been poisoned. Bogacki wasn't the kind of man anyone would bother to poison. He was a homeless man at the rotten end of a criminal career. If anything, we are dealing with a terrible accident. Our role is to work out how it happened and to ensure it doesn't happen to anyone else."

"I see." There was no arguing with Quigley.

She gave Diana a final smile and went to talk to a man in a hard hat. He must have had some role in the building work.

"You really saw him?" Carolyn said.

Diana looked at her. "The man? Yes." She could see tears brimming in Carolyn's eyes.

She squeezed her friend's hand. "You have a lot on your plate. You don't need to add the weight of the world to that burden. Are you done here?"

Carolyn looked around. "I guess so. It's just so sad that a man should die for no reason."

"Maybe I can treat us to lunch at the Guild cafeteria. Is the food as good as I remember?"

"That entirely depends upon how honest your memories are."

CHAPTER SIXTEEN

After a quiet and not entirely disappointing lunch with Carolyn, Diana approached the Clerkenwell Hostel on Farringdon Road. It was hidden away between a furniture shop and a Pret a Manger café, the only visible sign of its existence a ground floor doorway in a row of five-storey brown brick buildings.

She pressed the buzzer.

"Elroy," crackled the speaker, "I told you we're not open till four."

"Um, hello. I'm not Elroy," said Diana.

"We're still not open to guests until four."

"My name's Diana Bakewell. I wonder if you can help me?"

"What do you want?"

What *did* she want? The truth was simple and embarrassing. Her words to DS Quigley had fallen on deaf ears, her eyewitness account ignored. She *had* seen Marek Bogacki the night before he'd died. According to everything she'd heard, he should have already been dead. Her account didn't make sense... but it was important.

The voice on the buzzer changed to a woman's. "Diana? Is that you?"

"It is. Who's this?"

"It's Giselle Thompson."

It took Diana a moment to place the name and voice. She'd met Giselle many months earlier, at a protest camp in Parliament Square. Giselle had been part of a group protesting against 'fat cat' salaries and the injustices of poverty.

Before she could ask Giselle more, the door buzzed.

"Come up," said Giselle.

Diana entered. Inside was a steep, narrow flight of stairs leading to a first-floor office. It had been converted into a reception and communal area for the hostel. An older man sat behind the desk, exuding the air of someone who had been given a thorough kicking by life.

Coming round the desk, her head covered with a colourful scarf in Romany style, was Giselle. She beamed. "Diana Bakewell." She shook Diana's hand. "Clive. This is Diana. Proved a fellow campaigner's innocence in a nasty business at Westminster. Was that last year or the year before?"

"Time flies." Diana returned the smile. "You volunteer here now?"

Giselle laughed. "I run the place. I seem to have gone from fighting against injustice to pouring tea and filling in benefits forms for those who need it most."

"Practical work."

"Tiring work." Giselle went to a kettle balanced on a windowsill. "Coffee or tea? I've only got instant."

"Whatever's fine."

"I think we've got some of the cake left over from the ones

Jordan made, haven't we, Clive? Jordan is a resident. Used to be an army chef till it all went kaput for him. Wonderful baker."

Clive shuffled off. Giselle made tea while he searched for the cake.

"Not come to make a massive donation by any chance?" she asked.

"I haven't, although I'm happy to donate. I've actually come in search of information."

"Oh?"

"I'm looking for details on a man who might have stayed here. Marek Bogacki."

Giselle's hand wobbled as she spooned coffee granules into a cup. She laughed. "Oh, Marek, we know him well. Stayed here one night in three for months until a short while back."

"You know him, then? That's excellent. I'm looking for some background information."

"Why?"

There was no easy way to say this. "He's dead."

Giselle didn't respond until she'd put the lid back on the coffee. "I'm sorry to hear that. How?"

"He died at the hostel near St Paul's. It looks like he was poisoned."

"That's awful." The kettle clicked and Giselle poured. "It's funny."

"Funny?"

"So many people come through here. They leave and we never hear of them again. Ever. Then now and then the police or a solicitor turn up and tell us they've died. I don't know which is worse. To know someone is dead or to never know."

Clive returned with a Tupperware box. He peeled away the lid to reveal a selection of cream pastries.

"They look lovely." Diana sat down on one of the threadbare chairs around a wonky table.

"As I say, army chef. They don't mess about in the army."

Diana took a pastry and the mug of coffee.

"Marek," she said. "What do you know about him?"

"Polish by birth. Proper Cold War, behind the Iron Curtain Polish. I think he was a petty thief over there. Never caught, though. He came over here in the nineties and brought his skills with him. He was a burglar, then he began to specialise. He'd target highly valuable but poorly guarded items. He'd steal all the silver service from a big house or rip the paintings from the walls of a museum. He wasn't shy about telling us about his exploits, either. The man was unstoppable."

Clive scoffed.

"He was arrested?" Diana said.

Giselle nodded. "I think he went to prison twice. Once before we knew him. The second time... I'm not sure when. He came out maybe a year or more ago. He hadn't changed. He hadn't been looking after himself."

"Big chap," Diana said, remembering the fat man she'd seen at the upper floor window.

Giselle nodded. "Time living on the street ages you. He'd not been... yeah, he'd not been taking care of himself. He left here maybe a month ago. It'll be in the book. He'd fallen out with some residents. There were accusations of stealing."

"Because the man was a bloody thief." Clive's voice was bitter.

"Marek read the signs and decided to try resting his head somewhere else."

"St Paul's." Diana sipped her coffee.

"And he was poisoned, you say?"

"Organophosphate poisoning."

"What's that?"

"No idea. The police are investigating."

Giselle sucked in a breath. "I'm afraid to say he had plenty of enemies."

Clive sighed and Giselle turned to him.

"Clive, for the last time. No one stole your lucky pebble. You lost it. No one wants your pebble."

He shrugged. "How could I lose it? It was meant to be lucky."

Giselle looked at Diana. "Marek's eyes were always on a bigger prize. He was charming, made friends easily. But in the end, he made enemies just as quickly."

CHAPTER SEVENTEEN

ZAF AND JED sat down next to each other in the circle of chairs for the following morning's lesson.

Jed leaned towards Zaf. "You're early."

Zaf shrugged.

Parvani joined them. "Look at us, the early birds! First aid is being led by Doctor Blackthorn today. We must try to impress."

Zaf had only been early because right now, home was hell. Diana was still preparing to move out, and Alexsei had done nothing to stop his own father's lawyers pushing her from the flat.

"Are you going to try to impress Dr Blackthorn?" he asked Jed.

"I always impress," said Jed. "It's my natural manner."

"Mine too."

Doctor Blackthorn breezed in, two large black bags in tow. "First aid! Always a firm favourite, I find. It's all about taking action, which provides a relief to talking theory."

He placed the bags on the floor.

"We'll do resuss later in the day. First, let's practise applying dressings. Who's done this before?"

Most of the group raised a hand.

"It's like riding a bike, it will soon come flooding back."

By the time they all had their hands on the dressings, they were itching to get going.

"Practise on each other in your groups," said Blackthorn. "It's a skill that will improve every time you use it. Everyone do head injuries for the next fifteen minutes. Feedback to each other."

Jed applied a dressing and a bandage to Parvani's head. He stepped back and showed Zaf.

Zaf gasped, then laughed out loud. Jed had used the bandages to give Parvani bunny ears. He snapped a picture and showed it to her.

Her face creased into a scowl. The resulting picture was even funnier than the first impression, and Zaf hooted with laughter.

"What are you both doing?" Parvani hissed. "Don't you want to do well on this course?"

"We can do well and have some fun at the same time," Zaf said. "But I'm sorry Parvani. It was rude to laugh at you."

Parvani yanked the dressing off her head as Blackthorn looked up from some papers he was marking.

"Everything alright over there?" he asked.

"Yes," replied Parvani, then turned to straighten her hair. "Don't you want to win the prize for best group? Every intake has a contest, and you know Josephine will be all-out to make sure her group wins."

"What? First I heard of it," said Zaf.

"Me too," said Jed. "How is it awarded?"

"They take feedback from all lecturers and of course the

final project carries most of the marks. We need to start thinking about what ours should be."

Zaf and Jed glanced at each other. "Final project?"

"Let me bandage one of you and I'll tell you what I know." Parvani rolled her eyes.

The contest chat carried them through the lesson and out into the corridor. A barrier blocked the door to the Guild canteen.

"What's going on here?" Zaf said.

"Didn't you hear?" said Parvani. "I don't know if you two listen to anything. That man who died in the hostel..."

"Yes?"

"They think it was from the food he'd eaten that night."

"What?" said Jed.

Zaf remembered the dirty plate in the dead man's room. And the one hot food option available at the canteen that day.

"Shepherd's pie," he said.

With grated cheese on top.

Jed clutched his stomach. "Have we all been poisoned?"

Parvani shook her head. "If we'd eaten organophosphates in any meaningful quantity, we'd have been very ill a long time ago."

CHAPTER EIGHTEEN

The day on which Diana had to leave her flat finally arrived. She'd made enquiries, written letters and e-mails. None of it had changed anything. Zaf couldn't deny the flat was being taken from her.

Diana woke early.

She dressed and went out to walk around the square for the final time. As always, she picked up litter and watered the window boxes. Would someone else notice and take on the task after she was gone?

Nichola the gardener arrived as she finished. Diana waved and greeted her like it was any other meeting, knowing they wouldn't cross paths again.

She and Zaf shared a cup of tea before he had to leave for the Guild of Tourism. Zaf told her about the poisoned food at the Guild; she told him about the dead man, Marek.

Zaf looked at all the boxes and bags. "So Ernie's people are doing all the moving?"

Diana nodded. "He's got a moving business. They'll pack

everything up. I'll separate the things I want at mum's from the rest and they'll take care of it."

"There's only so much stuff you'll want at your mum's, given that it's temporary."

Diana smiled. Had she accumulated too much clutter in her life? Possibly. Did she love every single thing? Most definitely.

"Don't be maudlin for me, Zaf. I'll be fine at my mum's place. And you've got a place here with Alexsei."

"I'm... I'm not talking to that man, right now."

"Please don't blame him for what his dad and his dad's lawyers have done."

Zaf's face hardened. "I know he didn't make this happen, but he didn't stop it from happening, either."

Diana gave a sad shrug. "You two have made each other happy. Don't undo that. Your six-month anniversary is just round the corner. Find it in your heart to love him still."

"Oh, I love him. Just, right now, I'm not sure how much I like him."

After Zaf left, the movers arrived.

They worked for Big Ernie Holland, a man with more thumbs in dodgy pies than should have been possible. But they acted like consummate professionals.

Diana watched them wrap, pack, label and move box after box of her belongings. There would be breakages, confusion and things ending up in the wrong places, she was certain. But Ernie's team worked like a well-oiled machine and all she could do was stand by and watch.

She rode the seven miles east up front in one of the removal vans. They joined the Thames at Big Ben then carried on to the Tower of London before cutting north towards Spitalfields and then on through Whitechapel and Mile End.

Beverley Bakewell's flat was near the House Mill, a tidal mill dominated by the pointed roofs of oast house kilns. Diana hopped down from the van's cab and took in the view. She clenched a fist and told herself to be cheerful.

It would be nice to live by the water for a while, at least.

CHAPTER NINETEEN

Zaf looked around the re-opened cafeteria at the Guild of Tourism. It had been declared poison-free, but it was still empty. Not the best advert for the food.

Jed and Parvani were waiting for him in the college. As soon as he entered, they grabbed him and steered him back outside.

"We've got a session with Dr Blackthorn in five minutes," Zaf told them.

"Over at the crypt in St Paul's," Parvani replied. "We've got time. This is important."

"It's about the poison," Jed continued. "It was Parvani's idea."

"Poison?" Zaf said. "Did you know that Marek Bogacki was a convicted burglar?"

Jed looked at him. "What?"

"Diana told me. Bit of a sneak thief."

"Interesting. File that away for another time."

They marched him from the Guild entrance to the scaffolding and sheet-covered front of the hostel building. From within came the clanks, knocks and whirrs of industry.

Parvani pointed upwards. "This."

Zaf frowned. "Yes?"

"They're removing all the modern cladding from the building. Do you know why?"

He shrugged. "Thought it might be because it was like that terrible Grenfell Tower thing. Cheap and flammable."

"Organophosphates have been used to make insulating cladding."

"They made the cladding from poisonous chemicals?"

She nodded. "Organophosphate dust can be used as a flame retardant. The refurbishments here are because they were required to go with a safer option."

"So Marek's death might have been caused by exposure to the dust in the building."

Parvani shook her head. "It's hard to imagine how he would be exposed to enough of it to be poisoned."

"Would he have to eat it?"

"It can be absorbed through the skin. But unless he bathed in strong pesticides, I would say that ingestion is the most likely cause."

"You seem to know a lot about this."

"Chemical scientist at Imperial. You can't help but learn a few things."

Zaf looked at Parvani. Not only had she been in the building at the time of the murder, but she had a working knowledge of poisons.

They hurried over to St Paul's to join the rest of their class. They'd gathered by Nelson's tomb and were gazing at the huge marble structure.

"It's massive." Parvani pointed. "I don't know why anyone would need such a huge tomb."

"Have you seen Marx's?" Jed asked.

"No." Parvani looked round.

"It's not here, it's in Highgate Cemetery. But its scale is crazy big." Zaf used his arms to sketch out something the size of a truck.

A voice boomed from behind them. Zaf jumped. "You make a very good point. I like your style."

Dr Blackthorn grinned at their shocked faces. "Are we all here?" He did a headcount then led them away to a smaller exhibit. "Follow me, please."

The group trailed after him. "As you will have noticed," Blackthorn said as he strode, "the crypt here at St Paul's is unusually large. The largest crypt in Europe, in fact. It covers the same area as the Cathedral floor rather than just a small portion of it. Part of the reason for this is that when Wren built St Paul's, he was dealing with difficult conditions in the clay that lies beneath our feet. The huge stone piers you can see are carefully aligned with the pillars that hold up the dome upstairs."

They moved away from Nelson's tomb into a quieter area. "Here we have a small exhibit of relics from the old cathedral. Wren was charged with its restoration, which must have been quite a headache as it was apparently in very poor condition. The Great Fire of London took it away and presented Wren with a clean slate upon which he built the Cathedral in which we now stand."

Blackthorn gave a grand gesture to encompass the building, then swept his arm across to point into the cabinet against the wall. "The ruins smouldered for weeks after the fire was put out, and then of course the souvenir hunters descended. In some of your lifetimes you might remember a similar story when the Berlin Wall came down. It's a wonder that anything survived, but survive it did and you can see these treasures here in front of you. Anyone care to make any observations about what you see here? Architectural style?"

Among the jumble of fractured stone, Zaf could see design elements that echoed buildings he'd seen. A fragment of an arch, the lines from a pillar. "Is it gothic?"

"Show me."

Parvani pointed at the fragments of arch.

Blackthorn smiled. "Good work. Now I am about to show you some treasures that are not put out for display very often. It's not widely known that altar goods survived from Old St Paul's. Would you like to see them?"

"Yes," chorused the group.

Blackthorn led them over to another cabinet. "These were removed from the old cathedral at the time of the dissolution of the monasteries. They had been in hiding for a century when the great fire took place. This is a temporary exhibition, so you're very lucky. They're not always on display. Allow me to present to you the Ludgate candlesticks."

Zaf gazed at the pair of candlesticks. They were impressive, but not to his taste.

"Get closer, so that you can see the detail."

Josephine jabbed Jed with an elbow, making him yelp. Eventually they all settled into a semicircle and peered at the exhibits.

Each candlestick was nearly two feet tall with a wide base, a narrow stem and a flared top with a big spike for meaty church candles. What set them apart was the decoration. No part was undecorated. It wasn't like ornamentation stuck onto a solid base. Instead, the entire thing was made up of intertwined humans, foliage and flames and scenery.

"The Ludgate candlesticks date from the twelfth century," Blackthorn told them. "There was analysis performed on them in the nineties – which we were very lucky to be part of – that looked at the composition of the metal. It is all precious metal, with gold as the major component. But the proportions of those metals led scientists to believe that they were made from a hoard of old coins."

"Coins that were old in the twelfth century?" Zaf asked.

Blackthorn nodded. "Now, the method used to construct these was the lost wax method. Anyone heard of that?"

Nobody had.

"First, the design is created in wax. The mould is formed around it from something like clay. The melted wax escapes through vents and holes leaving a mould cavity into which your melted-down coins would be poured. Incredible, eh? Of course, Mr Strandman is the real expert on such things. You should ask Georg about it next time you're down here."

Zaf gazed at them, something tugging at his thoughts.

The dead man, Marek Bogacki, had been convicted for stealing antiquities. Was it simply coincidence that he was here at the time of this exhibition? It seemed unlikely.

"Are these very valuable?" he asked Blackthorn.

"Valuable? They are beyond value. The terms of their insurance mean that they must spend much of their time in a vault. The metal content alone is worth plenty, but when one adds in the historical context, the value to researchers and the craftsmanship, then their true worth is astronomical."

Zaf nodded.

"You reckon our dead burglar had been casing the joint?" Jed whispered to him.

Zaf laughed, then stopped. The thought had crossed his mind. Spooky.

CHAPTER TWENTY

Diana arrived at her mum's flat to find two men waiting outside. One was broad, the other was thin, and both were nearly hairless, though for different reasons.

"Uncle Ernie, Chaz," she said. "What are you two doing here?"

"Can't the management check up on their workforce once in a while?" Big Ernie replied.

"Dropped in on yer old mum for a cup of rosie," added Chaz.

Chaz Chase was Ernie's right-hand man, often his left-hand man too, a fixer of things, both legal and otherwise. He was also, on the side, a taxi driver, a pub landlord and generally a man whose fingers and thumbs were plunged into nearly as many pies as his boss.

Ernie gave a sideways nod at Chaz. "This one's been chewing my ear off about this new café he's bought in St John's Wood."

"Bistro eatery," Chaz said. "Called *Let it Bean*."

"Sounds like a café to me." Ernie clapped Diana on both

shoulders with his meaty hands. "I wanted to see how yer holding up."

"Oh. You know." She looked past him at her new home. "I've had it good for a long time. A new chapter starts today."

"Christ on a bike. That's you properly in the doldrums, then? Well the lads and laddesses should've taken proper care of all your stuff."

"I do worry about things being in storage, Ernie. Am I kidding myself that I'll ever be living anywhere big enough for it all again? Surely everything will have been eaten by rats before that ever happens."

"Oi! I'll have no talk of rats in my storage facility. You'll pop up again in some interestin' new way, you mark my words."

"Thanks Ernie, for everything."

A third figure now stood behind them. Beverley had shuffled to the front door of her flat to meet them.

"Who's this lot cluttering up my entrance?" she tutted.

"We'll be out of your hair in no time, Mrs B," said Ernie.

Diana went to her mum. Beverley was in her mid-eighties, and while it was impossible to hold back the years entirely, she was one of those fiercely active older people who was already sticking two fingers up to death and kept a cricket bat under her bed just in case.

She didn't hug Diana, but put a hand on her daughter's forearm.

"Let's not pretend this isn't a climb-down."

"Thanks, Mum."

"But it's only short-term. Now come in and let these hairy apes sort out your things."

Before she went inside properly, a thought occurred to her.

She turned back to Ernie. "Do you happen to know a man called Marek Bogacki?"

The two men smiled. "'Altar Boy' Bogacki?" said Ernie. "Yeah. In a manner of speaking."

"'Altar Boy'?"

"On account of his passion for robbing churches." He looked at Beverley and dropped the smile. "Unpleasant business. Affects the community, don't it?"

"Last I heard he was in Wandsworth," Chaz added. "B Wing, same as your mate."

"Morris Walker?"

"Yeah. Reckon they'd be neighbours."

"Marek got out a while ago," Diana remembered.

"Not long before he'll be back in again," Ernie said. "I can guarantee it."

I'm not so sure about that, Diana thought, but said nothing.

Soon enough, the movers had shifted everything and were on their way. And now Diana sat with her mum, surrounded by the boxes that were the bare minimum she needed to live. It was a crushing presence in the tiny flat, but her mum acted as if everything was fine.

"I made up the bed for you, and there's two empty drawers for you in the chest of drawers," Beverley told her.

Diana had brought her own bed linen, and the clothes that she had with her would need a lot more than two drawers, but she nodded in thanks. She was turning her mother's world upside down, and she needed to keep reminding herself of that.

"Made a mess, haven't I?" she said.

Beverley shrugged. "We'll sort it out when we have five minutes. What matters is that you've got a roof over your head. You wait, we'll be doing jigsaws and watching The Chase with our feet up in no time."

Diana put on a smile as she tried to picture herself doing those things, but inside she recoiled. She was used to having so much more space, and even with Zaf living under the same roof, if she'd felt like dancing to some cheesy eighties tunes, she was able to without disturbing him. This felt like camping.

But no, even that wasn't a decent comparison. Camping had always brought its own sense of freedom because the outside was right there. Here it was jigsaws and The Chase instead. It was going to take some getting used to.

There was a text from Newton on her phone.

Gus is very unhappy. Yowling all the time. I think he knows the company are going to sell off the buses.

Worried about his home. Diana knew how Gus felt.

CHAPTER TWENTY-ONE

Zaf had a bag in his hand. It wasn't everything he owned, but it was the gesture that mattered.

"I did have a home here. So did Diana."

Alexsei's heavy, dark eyes drooped with confusion and sadness. "I had nothing to do with this. I doubt even my father had anything to do with it."

Zaf shook his head. "Don't lie to yourself. You and your dad are big and powerful and I'm a nobody. My voice will never count for anything."

"You're not a nobody, Zaf. You're everything. I'm sorry."

"I'm not the one you need to apologise to."

"I didn't make Diana leave."

Zaf crossed his arms over his chest. "But you didn't stop the people who did make her leave."

Alexsei threw a hand out helplessly. "There are two empty flats up there now. Don't you see how foolish this is?"

Foolish, no. Painful, yes.

Zaf had never asked to live in the Eccleston Square house. He'd been grateful for the temporary measure, living rent free at first because Diana had taken pity on him and then because Alexsei, who only acted like a landlord when it suited him, had fallen for him.

He had no claim on any flat in the building, but he felt its loss nonetheless. It was a sign of how small he was compared to the Dadashov family.

"Where could you possibly go?" said Alexsei.

Zaf glared.

Alexsei realised his mistake. "I didn't mean—"

"Is that your argument? I should stay because I'm out of options? Am I your little toy boy?"

"There's barely any age difference between us."

Zaf spat out a bitter laugh. "Am I your *pet*?"

Alexsei recoiled. "Of course not."

"Of course not." Zaf turned away, mimicking Alexsei's tone. He was sinking to petty mockery now, but that was just a symptom of his hurt.

Alexsei ran a hand over his head. "Wait. Are you breaking up with me?"

Zaf's chest was tight. "I don't know."

"It's our six month anniversary meal in two days..."

"Is that a reason for us to stay together?"

"No. No. I love you, Zaf. Do you not...?"

Zaf closed his eyes. "I love you. I'm not sure I like you right now. I can't think straight. I'm just so angry. I need to go."

He turned away and let out his breath in a ragged sob of grief and fury.

Night had fallen. The air was warm. Zaf tried to calm himself, to breathe away the misery.

Where else could he go? He had friends, but apart from Alexsei and Diana, most of them were just passing acquaintances. Diana had her own accommodation issues and...

He needed to get away from Alexsei for a few nights to make his point. There was no point storming out if he came straight back.

Zaf couldn't afford a hotel. The other temporary sleeping alternatives he'd resorted to in the past, like kipping down at work or even hiding out in the shed in the Eccleston Square gardens, weren't options.

There weren't any options.

He laughed, despite his low mood. There was at least one option.

He walked to Victoria Station, caught the Circle Line to Mansion House and made the six-minute walk to the hostel by the Guild of Tourism. The reception desk was manned by the guy he remembered from the morning Marek Bogacki had been found, watching a TV show on his phone in an otherwise empty lobby.

Zaf cleared his throat. The guy jumped, yanked his earphones out and sat up. "Oh. Hello. Yes?"

"I'm a student at the Guild next door. Have you got any rooms available?"

Arpinder eyed the bag Zaf was carrying. "Now? You mean now?"

Zaf nodded.

"Did your girlfriend kick you out or something?"

Zaf wasn't going to correct him. "Do you have a room or not?"

Arpinder looked him up and down. "I need to know when you'll be paying."

Zaf's jaw clenched. He didn't have any money. Not until he got his next student loan payment.

He turned and walked out. The night air was cooler now. He stared up at the great dome of St Paul's, lit up silver grey.

Praying for divine help crossed his mind. But no. He knew what to do.

He phoned Diana.

"Oh, hello. Mum, can you turn the TV down? I can't hear him."

Zaf waited while the background noise reduced to a low babble.

"Phoning to check on me?" Diana asked.

"Phoning to ask a favour, actually."

"Who's that?" called Beverley.

"It's Zaf, Mum. What favour?"

"Is there… is there any chance your mum could put me up for the night?"

"What? What's happened?"

"What's he want?" called her mum.

"A place for the night, Mum. Zaf, did something happen between you and Alexsei?"

"I might have given him a piece of my mind."

Zaf heard Diana sigh. "Shot yourself in the foot with a grand gesture?"

"I was showing solidarity with a friend," he said.

"You can have the little room," Beverley said.

"What little room?" asked Diana.

"That little room."

"That's barely a cupboard."

"It's his if he wants it."

"I'll take it," Zaf said.

"You know the address?"

"Certainly do."

It was a walk back to Mansion House underground, and then a twenty minute ride to Bromley-by-Bow.

Zaf knocked on the door and went inside. He'd hardly

spent any time here. Bev had always come to their flat in London, or she and Diana had met up somewhere else. He hardly knew the woman.

"Hello Mrs Bakewell, I brought you some daffs." He held out a bunch of flowers he'd picked up at an all-night off licence.

Bev accepted them like he'd given her a diamond. "Oh, they're nice. Look at these, Diana. Thank you, Zaf. Diana's through here working on the jigsaw with me."

"Yay, jigsaw," Diana said.

"Come in. Pull up a chair. I hope you like steak and kidney pie, I've got one ready to go in the oven."

Zaf wasn't sure if Diana's enthusiasm about the jigsaw was genuine or not. He sat down and ate the pie.

When he'd finished, he felt awkward. "Shall I put my things in my room?"

"What room?" Diana said.

Bev waved a hand towards a door just off the entrance hall. It was a cupboard under the stairs. Zaf had seen plenty of them in films.

"Isn't that...?"

Diana nodded. "Yes. It's a cupboard."

Zaf opened it up. It was empty and clean. It had plenty of room for an airbed and a sleeping bag. And there was a shelf overhead which gave him enough space to stash his bags.

"Well, if it's good enough for Harry Potter..."

CHAPTER TWENTY-TWO

Diana headed to work the following morning. It had been a dead week at the Chartwell and Crouch depot. She had a couple of walking tours lined up for small groups, including another 'Swinging Sixties' tour of Carnaby Street and a more erudite 'Great Fire of London' tour later on.

Nonetheless, she notionally had a place of work she had to attend. And it was vital to everyone's sanity that she got out from under her mum's feet in the somewhat cramped flat. Beverley seemed delighted to have two house guests but Diana was feeling a little cramped already.

Inside the cavernous Chiltern Street depot, Newton looked uncomfortable in a shirt and tie. He kept running a finger around his collar as though he was being strangled.

"Oh my, Newton. What's this?"

"Shush, Paul will hear you. He's got someone here who's come to look at the buses. He made me dress up like this."

"Really?"

"Seriously, why would anyone imagine that mechanics look like this?"

"Well, drivers might look like that. Are you expected to take them out for a spin?"

"Oh wow, I hadn't thought of that. Yeah, maybe." Newton looked even more miserable.

"Shall I stick around?"

"No, you don't need to do that."

"It's partly selfish. I want to check up on the new owner, make sure they seem like a responsible person."

"Thank you. It would be nice to have some company."

It wasn't long before Paul Kensington emerged, all smiles as he guided his guest towards the buses. "Gentlemen, we have a potential buyer here to look over the buses. Tom, this is Newton, who's a whizz at keeping these beautiful vehicles in tip-top condition. Diana is one of our tour guides."

"We must have met in passing at some point," said Tom as he shook Diana's hand.

Tom Griffin was the owner of ACE Tours, manager to Ariadne Webb as Paul Kensington was to Diana. But the differences between Tom and Paul were many. Tom was clearly in his middle years but had a rugged physique, a head of thick chestnut brown hair and a complexion that suggested he spent a lot of time outdoors. In short, he looked like one of those Action Man toys from her childhood. By comparison, Paul Kensington was smaller, and the presence of Tom Griffin made his more rat-like attributes shine through.

"Diana, I hear your protégé Zaf Williams is on the same course as our Jed Skirmish. Hope they're enjoying their time at the Guild of Tourism."

"On company money," Paul pointed out.

"And every penny well spent."

"I'm sure, I'm sure."

"Are ACE Tours interested in our buses?" said Diana. "Your entire fleet is brand new."

"Diana, enough impertinence," said Paul.

"No, it's a fair question. I commend your insight. We at ACE are always looking out for new opportunities, and it's an open secret that these buses are some of the best examples of their kind. From what I gather, Newton has invested a lot of time and effort into making sure they're maintained in excellent condition."

Newton stood up straight with pride.

"Shall we take one of them for a spin?" said Paul Kensington. "Newton, would you take us out please?"

Newton obliged, and a few minutes later the four of them were aboard and pulling out into the morning traffic.

Diana sat towards the front out of habit, although she knew she wasn't required to act as a tour guide on this particular trip.

Tom studied the front of the bus, asking Newton endless questions about the power of the headlights, the maintenance schedule and the operation of the gears. He was being thorough.

There was a brief rattling sound. Tom looked down the bus. "What was that?"

"Oh that?" said Newton. "Well I'm not one of the ones that say the bus is haunted, but it does sometimes make noises like that. It's definitely not mechanical."

Diana raised her eyebrows.

Tom gave a small laugh. "I expect it's just a loose fitment."

"It. Is. Not. A. Loose. Fitment."

The rattling came again, as if it wanted to be part of the conversation.

"Oh." Paul couldn't bear it. "There are a dozen things it could be. Honestly, it's nothing to worry about."

Tom turned to him. "What are they, then, Paul? These things it could be?"

"Well. You know." Paul looked around at everyone as if it was obvious, but they were all waiting for him to continue. "It could be a cricket ball that someone left behind on the upper deck."

Diana and Tom stared hard at him. It was a peculiar thing to reach for.

"I clear every last speck of litter off the buses after they go out," called Newton from the front. "There is no way a cricket ball has been left behind by a passenger."

"No, of course not. It was just a 'for instance'."

The moaning started. Low, unhappy, wordless and inhuman.

"Is the bus haunted?" said Tom.

"No." Diana didn't want to scare him, or upset Newton. She got up and went over to one of the utility cupboards under the stairs. She opened the door and removed Gus the cat, who had been paddling his legs against the door as he sometimes did when bored. The moaning sound was unusual, though.

"I think this might be the culprit." She carried Gus over. "Our stowaway."

"How on earth do we keep letting that filthy thing on here?" Paul said.

Tom reached a hand over to stroke Gus. The cat normally leant into any affection offered, but this morning he seemed subdued.

"Well aren't you the most handsome cat?" Tom said. "If you are the resident ghost of this bus then I think we should all applaud your haunting skills."

"Adds charm and character," Paul said. "Buy the bus, you can have the cat for nothing."

"Over my dead body," muttered Newton.

CHAPTER TWENTY-THREE

The Guild students had an off-site lesson that morning. Zaf, Jed and Parvani climbed onto the coach as Georg ticked their names off a list. Georg followed them aboard once he was satisfied everyone was present and walked down the aisle.

Zaf watched Georg's face as it scrunched up in confusion. He looked up and down the coach and did a quick head-count. He leaned over to address someone sitting nearby. "Excuse me, where did you come from? I don't have you on my list."

"I'm one of the actors, Terry Rolls. The coach stopped to pick us all up before it came here. We will be acting as tour groups for your students."

"Ah, Terry! I'm sorry." said Georg. "I assumed we would meet you at the destination, but this is much better. Have you done this before?"

"Sure have! I like to think of my persona as the drunk tourist who won't do as he's told. It's a very convincing act."

Georg laughed. "Excellent. Well, it's important that the students gain experience in dealing with challenging clients."

Zaf turned to Jed on the seat beside him. "Real actors. We're doing live exercises with real pretend tourists."

"Out in the field, I know."

Parvani popped her head through the gap from behind. "Don't get giddy on me now. It's time to focus and shine, right, team?"

"Sure thing, Parvani." Jed gave Zaf a wink. "Although we can be a little bit giddy, can't we?"

Parvani rolled her eyes.

The coach pulled in at a bus stop on Park Lane and Georg took the microphone. "Now class, each group will be given a set of people who will be your tour group for today. You will go around the corner to Oxford Street and complete the tasks on the list you'll be given. Take pictures to demonstrate that you achieved each of these things, and we'll use them in the end of day round-up. Your group may include a variety of people, so your challenge today is to keep them all together and keep them safe in a very busy environment. Understood? We will meet back here at the end of the day, and please don't be late because the coach is not allowed to wait."

They filed off the coach and milled about on the wide pavement. Georg sorted them into groups, grumbling that he should have done it on the coach, because even here, away from the shops, it was very busy.

Fellow student Josephine barged a path through the crowd and corralled her group in front of a car showroom. She glanced across at Parvani's group as if she was afraid of being copied.

Parvani pulled her actors into line. She pulled a packet of coloured labels from her bag and stuck one onto each of them. "Welcome, everybody, you are part of the blue group. I am Parvani, this is Zaf and this is Jed."

There were ten people in their group, which Zaf thought should be very manageable. He shook the hands of each of them, looking them in the eye to commit their face to memory.

"Terry Rolls, occasional Colin Firth impersonator and stunt double for two series of *Snoop*!"

"A true celebrity walks among us," said Zaf.

Parvani read from the sheet that Georg had handed to her. "We need to guide the group to Marks and Spencer food hall where they will each buy themselves an apple, then we head to the Disney store where they will each be photographed trying on a hat but will not buy anything." She raised her head. "Sounds simple enough."

Jed leaned towards the group. "Are you allowed to share any details about the sort of person you'll be role playing?"

All of the actors looked back at him, stony faced.

"No? No." Jed turned to Zaf and Parvani. "We should assume they will all be difficult."

Parvani rolled her eyes. "No, Jed. We should assume good faith until we need to do otherwise. It's our job to treat them well and ensure they have a great day." She addressed the actors. "Can I please ask you to stay within sight of the group at all times? When we get onto Oxford Street it's going to be very busy. If anyone becomes separated from the group then our route takes us first to Marks and Spencer, followed by the Disney store, so —"

"Yay! Disney!" A woman split away from the group of actors and sprinted for the corner.

"Oh." Parvani looked at Jed and Zaf. "Do we go after her?"

"I think we know where we're going to find her," said Zaf with a shrug.

"But we need a photo of her buying an apple in Marks and Spencer," Jed pointed out.

Parvani bit her lip. "Do we go after her?" she repeated.

"If we split up now in an attempt to catch her, we'll likely create a bigger problem," said Zaf. "Let's take the hit and keep our cool, yeah?"

Parvani nodded, not looking happy. "Right. I will lead the way, Zaf and Jed will take up the rear. We walk directly to Marks and Spencer, no stopping or diverting, clear?"

Zaf was automatically watchful. He had no doubt these pretend tourists had surprises to spring on them.

CHAPTER TWENTY-FOUR

PAUL LED Tom Griffin from the bus and laid a companionable hand on the other man's shoulder as the two of them walked over to the office to discuss 'the deal' further.

"Don't let go of him," said Newton.

Diana had the lethargic Gus in her arms.

"That moaning he was doing on the bus," she said. "That's not normal."

Gus shook his head. "He's been really off. Hasn't eaten, hasn't been playing with his usual toys. If I was a fanciful man—"

"Which you're not."

"– then I'd say he was worried about us selling off the buses. He loves them, he does."

"Is it something he's eaten?"

"Possibly. You getting out all those boxes might have exposed some horrid thing in a corner that he's eaten."

She stroked the cat. "But you're not blaming me."

"Oh, no. He had that whole phase of stealing shoes from across the road. He could have eaten a shoelace. He's got a vet's appointment, so if you hold onto him while I get the cat carrier..."

"Not a problem. Need company to the vets?"

"I wouldn't say no." Newton rushed to the storage cupboard.

There was a silhouette in the depot's open vehicle door. Two silhouettes. One was tall and broad-shouldered, almost rectangular. The other was much smaller. Only when they stepped fully into the building and out of the light did Diana see it was Detective Sergeant Quigley, now accompanied by her senior officer, Detective Chief Inspector Clint Sugarbrook.

Diana stroked Gus's thick fur theatrically.

"Ah, Mr Sugarbrook, so glad you could join me."

"Pardon?" said Sugarbrook.

"I was doing my James Bond villain impression. This is Gus."

"We've met."

"Apologies for the silliness. I'm holding him for a friend."

"I see."

Diana Bakewell had met DCI Sugarbrook on numerous occasions, ever since their first encounter at a crime scene in the Palace of Westminster. She had even sought him out a few months back regarding a murder she'd witnessed aboard a boat on the Thames. It was her impression that he regarded her as a nuisance, an interfering busybody, although he never referred to her as such. It was not like him to seek her out without great cause.

"How are you and all the little Sugarbrooks?" she asked.

"Can't complain."

"Actually, he can," said DS Quigley.

"The dog," grunted Sugarbrook.

"What dog?" Diana asked.

Sugarbrook eyed her. "The dog you retrieved from that houseboat. He's with my family now."

Diana smiled. She'd found the dog while investigating the murder she'd witnessed from the London Eye. "JMW Turner," she said.

Sugarbrook grunted again. "I made the mistake of taking him home, just for one night. My girls fell in love with that darned thing."

"Oh."

"So now we have a dog."

Diana jiggled Gus in her arms. "Animals do have a habit of worming their way into our affections."

Newton was returning with a bright pink plastic cat carrier. Gus didn't squirm or try to escape at the sight of it, which suggested he was truly unwell.

"We were just off to the vets," explained Diana.

"I wondered if I might have a word," said Sugarbrook.

"Yes?"

"About the death of Marek Bogacki."

"We're off to the vets."

"Which one?"

"Connaught Street Vets near Hyde Park," said Newton.

"Quigley can drive us all over there and we can talk."

DS Quigley didn't seem enthralled by the idea, but she was the sergeant and he was the chief inspector.

"Fine by me," said Newton, who would have had to walk or take a taxi there otherwise.

"Maybe Diana can help me unpick some impossible questions."

CHAPTER TWENTY-FIVE

Zaf eyed the fake tour group as they set off down the street. He could see immediately what was going to happen. Parvani was only slightly below average height, but even assuming the actors were planning to behave themselves, they couldn't do anything about the fact that she'd almost immediately disappeared into the crowd.

"Two ticks, I need to fix this!" Zaf shouted to Jed. He stopped at a booth selling souvenirs. Everything that could be emblazoned with a union jack was there, displayed for maximum gaudy attention.

"Umbrella please!" Zaf said to the seller, pointing. A moment later he was in possession of an umbrella. He sprinted ahead and found Parvani. "Hold this up, they can't see you."

"Oh. Thank you!" She held it aloft and Zaf trotted back to join Jed, updating the group members as he went.

"If I have learned anything from Diana, it's the value of an umbrella. Have we lost anyone?"

Jed pointed at a woman with red hair. "That one there

keeps trying to sneak into shops. I've fetched her back every time so far, but she's a slippery one."

Zaf and Jed continued their eagle-eyed watch over the group, taking it in turns to retrieve the dawdlers and would-be absconders.

Zaf smiled as they walked past Selfridges, thinking of the art deco brasserie restaurant on its upper floor and a delightful lunch Alexsei had treated him to a couple of months back.

There had been a string of messages from Alexsei overnight. Only one was an apology. Maybe Alexsei had too much pride for more than that. Maybe he knew that grovelling was never going to be a good look. The other texts had all been hints at the plans Alexsei had made for their anniversary meal. It might have seemed a shallow and obvious gesture, but Alexsei knew Zaf. Principled indignation at Diana's eviction was one thing but Zaf loved a classy night on the town, especially if he was being treated.

When the tour group arrived at Marks and Spencer's food hall Parvani did a headcount and was impressed to find that the only person missing was the Disney-obsessed woman. "Apples then, everybody." She shepherded them over to the fruit display. "It specifically says that everyone is supposed to buy their own. Let's take an apple each and head for one of the self-service checkouts, shall we?"

Parvani led the way and the actors formed a queue at the checkouts.

"Right, I need to take a picture of each of you buying an apple," said Parvani. "Use my debit card, and as you finish, pass it to the person behind. When you have your apple, come and stand behind me."

"What do you want us to do, Parvani?" asked Jed.

"You want an apple? Get at the back of the line," said Parvani.

Zaf and Jed each took an apple and joined the queue. It was slightly tedious as each person made their own transaction.

"Surely we could have put the apples all through in one payment and just posed everyone in front of the checkout?" whispered Jed.

"I think Parvani wants to do things by the book," Zaf replied.

Eventually it was their turn, and they put three apples through in a single transaction, took one each and handed the third to Parvani.

"Nice work!" said Zaf.

Parvani turned to the group. "Quick headcount, then it's off to Disney. Wait, we're down by two. Who's missing?"

"Sorry, we're right here!" called Terry Rolls as he and another of the actors emerged from behind a customer service desk with an enormous box.

For a few long moments, Parvani was lost for words. "What on earth have you got there?" she asked, finally.

"It's just an armchair I had on order. Thought I might as well pick it up while we're passing through," said Terry. "My mate Billy said he'd help me carry it."

Zaf wasn't sure what size armchair it might be, but the box was nearly as tall as Terry. It made it impossible to see who stood on the other side of it, and had already started to create congestion as people tried to walk past.

"Would you say that box is empty?" Jed whispered. "They don't seem to be having much trouble carrying it."

Zaf studied Terry's movements. "You're right. It looks as light as a feather. It's a set-up, isn't it? They stall us here processing these apples one at a time and then they introduce a giant box that will hamper our progress."

"So what do we do about it?" Jed asked.

"I'm not sure there's much we can do," said Zaf. "We just keep smiling and carry on."

Zaf approached Parvani and gave her a discreet nudge. "We think the box is empty. It's one of the challenges, see how we cope."

"It's very immersive," said Jed, impressed despite the imposition.

Parvani nodded. "Makes sense. We may have to try something different." She raised her voice to address the actors. "We have to get to the Disney store now. In order for us all to stay together, I am going to suggest that we have Terry and Billy in front and that we all follow, holding hands."

There was a loud rumble of disapproval from the crowd. Zaf couldn't pick out any specific voices, but he had the distinct impression that the rumbling amounted to a collective unhappiness at the idea of holding hands.

Parvani badgered the group, one at a time, and as they left the shop they were all holding hands. As soon as her back was turned, everyone let go and shuffled forward, brimming with resentment at the invasion of their personal space.

Out on the street, the giant television box was even more of a liability than Zaf had imagined. Every group they encountered trying to walk together in the opposite direction was split in half by the box. They couldn't get back together because of Parvani's human chain, and so people became angry and panicked, especially if it was a family who were trying to keep hold of their children.

Zaf spent a lot of time apologising to people who didn't

appreciate it. He was rapidly coming to the opinion that this training activity was less an educational exercise, and more some perverse initiation into the world of tour guiding.

CHAPTER TWENTY-SIX

"Can't tell you much you don't already know," said DCI Sugarbrook to Diana.

The two of them sat in the back of Quigley's unmarked police car. It was a big car but Sugarbrook still looked awfully squashed in the back seat. Quigley was driving and Newton sat up front with Gus in his cat carrier.

Usually, Gus loved travel. He enjoyed nothing better than spending a day on a tour bus doing circuits of London. Even now, when clearly under the weather, he was keen to see where he was going. Newton raised his knees and propped the carrier on them like he was an observation platform from which Gus could look out of the windows and survey his city.

"Mark Bogacki died more than a week ago," said Sugarbrook. "At first we thought it might have been a drug overdose, maybe a diabetic coma. Then it was determined to be organophosphate poisoning."

Diana nodded. She knew this bit.

"The building he was in was being renovated. The exterior

cladding panels were being removed. They contain organophosphates. I asked Quigley to find out if someone had been careless during the works, maybe even killed the man on purpose."

"But that wasn't how it happened," said Diana.

"The poison was in his food, the last meal he ate. It had come from the canteen of the Guild of Tourism next door."

"Shepherd's pie."

Zaf nodded. "It was the only option that day. Bogacki took the meal to his room, ate it and, less than an hour later, he was dead. He might have felt ill, the pathologist said, but it wouldn't have been a violent death. He could have cried out in distress. Or he might have just taken himself to bed, thinking he had a sudden fever, and slipped away."

"Small mercies."

"We thought maybe some of the renovation stuff had got into the kitchen. That place is a managerial mess."

"Is it?"

"It's struggling financially."

Diana hadn't known that. The image of Carolyn Desanti's desk, piled high with paper, and the stress in her voice when she talked about work, came to mind.

"They were having to make cuts," Sugarbrook said. "Pay cuts, redundancies. If I understand your work situation well enough, I think you know what I mean."

Diana nodded.

"In that kind of environment, mistakes are made. But we checked the kitchens. There was no sign of contamination. The kitchens were clean."

"Which means..."

Sugarbrook nodded. "Which means..."

Diana raised an eyebrow."Unless it was an unusual form of

suicide, someone sprinkled this stuff on Marek Bogacki's shepherd's pie."

"Quite."

"You have a murder on your hands," Diana told the DCI.

"And it's a very strange one."

"Surely that's common in your line of work."

"Not a murder like this."

"We're here." Quigley parked the car outside a vet's clinic with a white front. One advantage of being a police detective was you could park anywhere.

Newton struggled to get out with the carrier on his knee. Diana jumped out, ran to his door and took Gus while Newton got out. Casual shoppers were wandering up and down the small parade of shops, enjoying the sunshine. The Le Pain Quotidien café across the road was doing a brisk trade.

"Quigley can help Mr Crombie get the cat into the vet," said Sugarbrook.

"Can I?" Quigley didn't wait for an answer, just followed Newton and the cat carrier inside.

Now Diana and Sugarbrook were alone on the pavement. The vet clinic had large windows; from outside it looked light in there, and warm. A bell jingled as someone entered the shop next door.

"There are two odd things about Marek Bogacki's death," Sugarbrook said.

"Are there?"

"First, he was probably moved after he died."

"What?"

"Your young friend Zaf was in there and then the paramedics arrived..."

"Yes..."

"...while rigor mortis was present. Possibly. It's something to do with how the blood pools in the body. The pathologist isn't sure but thinks maybe."

"Is there no CCTV in the hostel?" she asked.

"Only in the lobby. And it wasn't working that night. The hostel is run by the Guild with funding from St Paul's. Between the chaos caused by the renovations and the state of the Guild, there's not much organisation. The receptionists can't even confirm if the lobby was fully manned."

"So it's possible someone came in while Marek was dead. Robbery?"

"That did cross our minds. But what would an old homeless man have that was worth stealing? His rucksack was packed and unopened."

Diana eyed him. "You didn't know about his past?"

Sugarbrook shifted his weight. "His past?"

She nodded. "He was a notorious antiquities thief." She watched the DCI for a reaction.

"Hmm." He eyed her. "You know about that."

So he did know. And he hadn't wanted to tell her. Interfering busybody was how Sugarbrook saw her. Sometimes, at least.

There was a moment's silence. If they'd foind anything on Marek, Sugarbrook wasn't about to tell her.

"But still he was moved," she said. "Odd."

"Exactly."

Through the window of the vets, Diana could see Newton talking to the woman at the counter.

"And then there's the other post-mortem peculiarity," Sugarbrook said.

"Yes?"

"You gave a witness account that you saw Marek Bogacki in the hostel."

"I did."

"As you were passing by in the churchyard below. And you were adamant it was nine o'clock."

"I looked at the clock above the Guild door. It said nine o'clock."

Sugarbrook pulled his lips back. "Yeah, that's the problem."

"The coroner or pathologist thinks he died before that, I suppose?"

"Doesn't think it. Is certain. Time of death is being put before seven pm. I have been told in no uncertain terms that even eight pm is outside the realms of possibility. Nine? No. Just can't be the case."

"What can I say except that I saw what I saw? I am not a liar. I am not, as Newton would put it, a fanciful person."

"No, you're not." There was regret in Sugarbrook's voice. "Which means, Miss Bakewell, you saw a man up and about two hours after he had died."

CHAPTER TWENTY-SEVEN

ZAF LET OUT a breath as the tour group finally arrived at the Disney store.

The store was busy and full of shiny, colourful things. Zaf's little sister would have loved it.

Parvani gathered the group together for a headcount. It was awkward, with the enormous box. Wherever Terry and Billy put it down, it blocked people from looking at the shelves.

She noticed the problem too. "Zaf, would you please see if you can find the woman who ran away when we got off the coach?"

"On it."

Zaf dodged round a family examining a rack of t-shirts and spotted the woman. She was twirling in front of a mirror, trying on a sparkly cape and tiara. "Looks good."

She started. "Rest of group here now?"

Zaf nodded.

With a toss of her head, the woman joined the rest of the group. Parvani beamed at Zaf from beside her line of actors.

"Someone grab a hat. We'll pass it down the line and get a picture of everyone trying it on."

"Wait, no," said the woman with the tiara. "I've got my own hat."

"Fine." Parvani snapped a picture with her phone. "Rest of you, hat please."

"I want to start, then I won't catch their nits." Terry jammed a Micky Mouse Fantasia hat onto his head. It had mouse ears and a wizard's hat.

Zaf thought it suited him.

After Parvani had her picture, Terry passed the hat along the line. Billy hesitated. "I don't want nits."

"I haven't got nits, mate, but I don't know about everyone else."

Zaf couldn't tell if Terry was joking or not.

Or cared.

The group were arguing about headwear.

"Can we get away with using a filter to add the hats?" Jed was already moving down the group, snapping pictures that added pirate hats to everyone. "I mean, we're obviously in the Disney store. If anyone asks, tell them there were hygiene concerns."

Parvani winced.

Zaf thought it looked better with the group distracted, and there were definitely fewer people tutting at them.

"Come on," Parvani said. "Shall we take a walk back to the coach? All we have to do is make sure we don't lose anyone."

She led them out of the store onto the busy pavement.

An alarm beeped behind them.

They always seemed to be going off in shops.

Or did they?

A security guard rushed up to the woman with the tiara

and sparkly cape. "Excuse me, madam. Can I please check whether you've paid for those items?"

She bit her lip. "Sorry. I..." She looked at Zaf. "I forgot I was wearing them."

While the woman went back inside to pay, Zaf moved the group to one side so as to block less of the pavement with the box.

"Oh, hey." Jed pointed to the opposite pavement. "It's Josephine's group. What are they doing?"

Zaf looked.

Josephine, along with her two helpers Sacha and Adi, had linked arms in a V formation, and the three of them were bellowing at pedestrians to clear a path.

One man had been pushed into the road.

"She's a monster," Zaf said.

"A monster who's making better progress than us." Jed raised an eyebrow. "They've got one of those big boxes as well, but look at them move. We'll be back in a few minutes. Leave them to it."

When Josephine's human bulldozer had forced enough people out of the way, Zaf and the rest of his group slipped past and hurried back to the coach.

Zaf sank into his seat.

At last.

The box was in the luggage space beneath the coach and everyone was on board. The actors were talking about their performances and Zaf couldn't help listening.

"I do always enjoy the reveal, that special moment when we turn up with the box," Terry was saying. "I think it worked especially well in the new location by the self-checkout. I heard there's a bigger chair available. Can you imagine their faces?"

Zaf didn't have to imagine.

They pulled up outside the Guild and gathered in a classroom for a debrief.

Georg stood at the front, flicking across the screen of a tablet. "I believe I have all of your submissions now. And the feedback from the actors, of course. Let's examine what went well. Josephine, your group achieved all of its target outcomes. I don't think you dropped any marks there. Parvani, well done on exploring ways of keeping the group together.

"Where do we need to deduct points? In terms of completeness, Parvani, your team lost marks because you didn't get an apple picture with everyone. The actor who ran away was separated from the group for too long. A deduction will be made."

Zaf gave her an encouraging smile. This wasn't X Factor. Georg couldn't send her home.

Josephine was another matter.

She had her arms folded and was wearing a scowl that could curdle milk.

"Josephine, your group chased down their runaway, although a rugby tackle was perhaps too forceful. You also engaged in some unacceptable bullying of the public."

"What?"

Georg cleared his throat. "I am a new member of the teaching faculty here. There are..." He tailed off, as if he didn't want to say what Zaf was thinking. "I think it is possible that, given the nature of these groups, you might return with fewer 'tourists' than you started with."

"I didn't lose anyone."

"No, not at all. You achieved what I assume is an absolute first. You returned to the coach with one more tourist than you left with. Poor Mrs Astrakhan was most upset."

"That's not my fault."

Georg didn't look like he was expecting an apology.

Zaf couldn't help feeling pleased. There was no way Josephine would have realised she'd picked up an extra tourist.

"So on balance," Georg said, "the winner of today's challenge is Parvani's group. Well done."

Parvani let out a whoop.

Zaf and Jed grinned at each other.

Take that, Josephine.

After the lesson had broken up, Zaf hung back to talk to Georg.

He had an idea forming, a theory. But he needed to run it past someone with more experience.

"Sir, can I ask you a question?"

"Of course." Georg sat back in his chair. "Ask away."

"It's about the Ludgate Candlesticks. Doctor Blackthorn showed them to us, they're amazing. They're in the Cathedral for a special display. I found out the man who died in the hostel was known to the police for stealing artifacts. Is it possible he was here to steal the candlesticks?"

Georg nodded. "That's an interesting idea."

"Or is it bonkers?"

Georg stroked his bearded chin. "The Ludgate Candlesticks, you say? I must make an effort to go and see them while they're on display." He scrunched up his face in thought. "Valuable artifacts will draw the attention of unscrupulous people. The question is whether this idea is useful in the context of the man's death. Perhaps it is. In which case, you should inform the police."

CHAPTER TWENTY-EIGHT

Newton Crombie had disappeared somewhere inside the vets with Gus, and apparently, he'd taken DS Quigley with him. Diana didn't imagine she'd expected to be attending to a yowling cat when she picked up her detective's badge that morning.

Sugarbrook leaned against the police car.

"So, I need to ask," he said, "are you one hundred percent certain about what you saw?"

Diana thought about it. She'd seen a man. Big. Grey beard. Dressed like a homeless man. Even from the distance she could see the creases and dirt in his long clothes. He wore an orange knitted hat. The clock said nine o'clock.

"I saw him," she said. "That was Marek Bogacki."

"But given what we know, some part of the scene you have described was impossible. But we don't know which."

"It just doesn't make sense," Diana said.

"I know."

"Marek Bogacki was a criminal. It must be relevant."

Sugarbrook gave her a look and cleared his throat. "He was a burglar. At his height he was stealing big ticket items or historical curios. Eight years ago, he broke into the Pathology Museum at Imperial College London and stole several anatomical specimens. Bizarre. No idea where he intended to sell them."

She nodded. "But maybe, over his career, he made enemies."

Sugarbrook grunted. "Maybe. But he was sixty-six, a has-been."

"Excuse me?"

He gave her a smile. "You're in your prime, Miss Bakewell. You'll be harrying me right up until my retirement date. But Bogacki... Ask the criminal fraternity about Marek Bogacki and the majority of them will shrug their shoulders and say 'who?' No, I don't think I'd even know who to ask about that aspect of his life."

A thought struck Diana. She did know someone who might have known Marek Bogacki more recently: Morris Walker in Wandsworth jail.

She didn't mention it to Sugarbrook. He didn't need to know everything.

There was movement inside the vets and Newton and Quigley emerged with Gus in the cat carrier. Newton had a puzzled expression.

"You'll never guess what," he said.

"What? Is it serious?"

"That very much depends on how you look at it," said Newton.

"Come on, Crombie," said Quigley.

"Your cat eats too much," Diana guessed.

"No, well, yes. But it's not that simple."

"He's been doubling up on dinners," added Diana, thoughtfully.

"That he has. The vet scanned him for his microchip and brought up his records. Turns out someone had brought him in only two weeks ago."

"Someone?"

"A family on George Street. Turns out Gus has been spending many of his nights at their residence."

"They call him Tiger," added Quigley, "which is obviously the wrong name for this chap."

"And they've been treating him like he was their cat."

Diana could see where this was going.

"Slipping from house to house under a false identity."

"Can cats have a fake identity?"

Newton frowned. "One can't help but feel a sense of betrayal."

In the cat carrier, Gus curled up, entirely unrepentant.

CHAPTER TWENTY-NINE

When Zaf's lessons for the day were finally over, Diana was waiting for him outside.

"I wasn't expecting to see you today."

She raised an eyebrow. "We currently live together. You have the tiniest bedroom known to man."

He grinned. "True. Although I should have a space at this place" – he gestured to the hostel – "by the end of the week."

"You got time for a walk and a talk?"

He rubbed his eyes. "It's been a long day. A long, tiring and weird day. And Alexsei and I have our anniversary meal tonight."

"You're still going ahead with that."

It was a statement, not a question. Within it there was a note of approval.

"I'm still very angry."

She nodded.

"You learn eventually," she said, "that all of life is built on compromise. Friendships, relationships, goals, dreams... they're never clean, clear or beautiful. There's always some mud in the mix."

"Never cut your nose off to spite your face." He frowned. "I never understood that saying. How do you even spite your own face? But, yes, a walk. And a talk."

"I have things to ask." She narrowed her eyes. "Shall we take a wander through the Cathedral or have you had enough of the place?"

"Get tired of the landmarks of London?"

She smiled.

In the late afternoon, the Cathedral was relatively quiet. There were still tourists about, but there was also a noticeable number of people coming into the building for personal reflection and in preparation for the evening service.

"A brisk walk up to the Whispering Gallery?" Diana suggested.

They crossed the nave, beneath the high and colourfully decorated dome to the stairs by the south transept. Through a door were the stairs leading up to the dome. By the entrance was a sign giving all the usual warnings about who should and shouldn't tackle the two hundred and fifty nine steps from the ground to the Whispering Gallery. The spiral steps were broad enough for people to walk four abreast, and Zaf and Diana walked up side by side. As they did, Diana told him about a visit she'd had from DCI Sugarbrook that day and the questions he had put to her. When she mentioned the stolen anatomical specimens as an example of his eclectic crimes, Zaf had to double check.

"Imperial College?"

"Yes? Is that important?"

"No. I don't think so. But it's a strange turn up for the books if old Sugarbrook is asking you for help."

She smiled. "I think he was hoping I'd change my statement and say I was entirely mistaken about what I saw that night. Something clearly doesn't add up. I was wondering..."

"Yes?"

"If someone had been tampering with the clock at the Guild. What if – and I don't really understand why – what if someone wanted there to be a witness to Marek being alive and had altered the time. I don't see how or why..."

"This the big clock over the door?"

"Yes."

The clock above the entrance to the Guild of Tourism was more like a church clock than anything a normal building might have on its wall. It's face was composed of metal pieces over a coloured glass background.

"The mechanism would be inside the building," Zaf said. "Maybe in a cupboard on the first floor."

"You could have a look, couldn't you?"

Zaf grinned. "Trying to get me into trouble. Is that what the old girls of the Guild do? Try to lead young students astray?"

"It would put my mind at ease."

"Of course."

They reached the level of the Whispering Gallery. It was no gallery in the sense that Zaf understood, but a walkway running round the inside of St Paul's enormous dome. Through high protective railings, he could see across the breadth of the dome and down to the floor of the Cathedral. It was a space in which one could truly get a grasp of the scale of the place, and it made his stomach feel weird.

"Is it true?" he asked.

"Is what true?"

"That if you stand on one side and whisper, the sound is carried to the far side?"

"I've never known St Paul's quiet enough to test it."

This was the first of three galleries. There was the Stone Gallery further up on the outside of the dome and the Golden Gallery on the very top by the cross. Carolyn Desanti had taken them up the five hundred and eighty-two steps to the very top in their first week. It was a vertigo-inducing trek that Zaf did not intend to repeat unless strictly necessary.

"We've been working on a theory," he said, as they looked out at the religious paintings that adorned the inside of the dome.

"We?"

"Me and Jed and Parvani."

"I'm glad you've made friends. What theory?"

"What if Marek had been at the hostel because he was casing this place?"

"Casing?"

"As in casing the joint. What if he had been planning to steal something from the Cathedral?"

"Audacious."

"I didn't say he was a sensible burglar."

"What would he have stolen?"

"There's the Ludgate Candlesticks in the crypt. The gold cross on the altar there. Everywhere you look there's valuables. They've got that famous Jesus painting somewhere."

"The Light of the World by William Holman Hunt."

"That'd be worth thousands."

"Possibly more," Diana agreed. "And I suppose Marek would have planned to walk out with a life-size painting of Jesus Christ tucked under his arm?"

"It's all part of a general theory."

Diana stretched her neck and yawned.

"That could be possible, or it could simply be that an old Polish émigré needed a bed for the night. And even if he was here to steal something, why would that have anything to do with him being poisoned while staying at the hostel?"

"Someone could have murdered him to stop him carrying out the theft."

"Seems unlikely."

"Or... or someone killed him to stop him carrying out the theft before they did."

"Excuse me?"

"You know. Someone knew Marek Bogacki was going to steal the valuable thing but they had already planned to steal it themselves. How to stop the competition getting there first? A bit of horrible poison stolen from the renovation works next door and sprinkled onto his shepherd's pie."

"Do you think that might be what happened?"

He thought about it. "No. But it might be something like that. Whatever's happened, someone wanted Marek dead."

CHAPTER THIRTY

When Diana arrived at her mum's flat that evening she was shocked all over again by the cramped mess her own arrival had made of the place. Even though she was the one who'd made it happen, she hadn't yet fully absorbed the awfulness of it.

"In here, love!" called Bev.

It made Diana smile. Where else could her mother be? It was such a tiny flat.

Diana could hear voices, and wondered who was here. She went through to the lounge. Nobody was there except her mum, who slightly reduced the volume on a digital speaker.

"Audiobook," Beverley explained. "You can get them from the library. Jigsaws too! I try and theme them. Take a pew and see what you think. It's a jigsaw of Regency England and the book is Pride and Prejudice. It's halfway through but I expect you know the story already. You'll soon get the gist."

Beverley turned the volume back up, crushing any possibility of conversation. Diana sat, trying to find enjoyment. It sounded like Rosamund Pike narrating the story, which was probably lovely at normal volume, but it was hurting Diana's ears. She resolved to get Bev's hearing checked out.

"I'm going to see Morris Walker tomorrow," Diana said.

"What?" Bev shouted.

"I'm going to see—"

"You'll have to speak up."

Diana reached over and turned off the audiobook.

Beverley sighed. "It's the bit where they're all mooning around over Wickham. Annoying when you know what's coming up. Anyway, what were you saying love?"

"Morris Walker."

Beverley frowned. "Oh, him. But he's in prison, isn't he?"

"Wandsworth."

Bev's lip curled. "Rubbish selection in their hot drink vending machine."

"What?"

"Used to visit your Great Uncle Noaksie there."

Diana had the vaguest recollections of an uncle she'd never really known. It was no surprise that there were members of the Bakewell family that been in prison.

"You were sweet on him once, weren't you? Back in the day?" said Bev.

"Morris? Me? I don't think so."

"I remember it differently," said Bev. "That business with him going to prison. I always had the feeling you thought it weren't right, though."

"No, it wasn't right. It still isn't right."

"Tell me."

"Well there were definitely dodgy dealings," said Diana, wrinkling her nose. "There was a website, set up in the name of Chartwell and Crouch. It sold tickets that never existed.

Hundreds of them got sold before it was closed down, a load of money went into a bank account that had Morris's name on it."

"But he was the manager of Chartwell and Crouch."

"Yes, but this wasn't the official site. The police case was built on the notion that Morris had built this dummy website that looked like the company he worked for, but it sold non-existent tickets and just dumped the money in a personal account of his. They said he was defrauding the public and tarnishing the name of his own company."

Beverley nodded. "The police can trace those things, can't they?"

"They can, and they did. This is where it gets hard to explain. That account was cleared out, all the money was withdrawn in one go, just before it all came crashing down."

"Right. I've watched telly, love. Money *always* leaves a trail."

"They had experts look at it and their findings were 'inconclusive'."

"Well we all know what that means then, don't we?" said Beverly. "We're all innocent until proven guilty. If it's inconclusive then how did they send him down?"

"Because they said he lied about his alibi. Morris insisted he couldn't have been at the bank when the withdrawal happened because he'd been in this café all afternoon. He stuck to that."

"And? Wasn't he there?"

"Not only was he not there, but the details he gave about the place didn't match." She reached into her handbag and pulled out the letter she had received from Morris a couple of weeks back. "He writes. I sometimes write back. I visit him when I can." Diana unfolded the letter. "He's given me more details about the café. Years later, he's still giving details. This café round the corner from the Best Western Hotel on Sussex Gardens, up from Hyde Park. He went there to write."

"Write?"

"Apparently he was still penning songs. The man always had music in his heart. And in his account, he mentions what he had – mushroom and ham bruschetta – and this encounter with a little woman and her dog, a Pomeranian. Here, he recalls its name: Marengo. Marengo the dog. Super specific details."

"Sounds like a tight alibi."

Diana shook her head. "He never changed his story. It was his undoing, because they said if he'd lied about that then why wasn't he lying about everything else? And because he claimed no knowledge of it, he wasn't able – or willing – to give them the hundreds of thousands of pounds of stolen money back. It never turned up. Chartwell and Crouch ended up footing the bill for most of it."

"Flipping 'eck," said Bev. "What's the answer, then?"

"Never got to the bottom of it, Mum. I really wish I knew."

Beverley leaned across, and Diana thought she was about to offer some insight that would help to free Morris. But she had spotted the correct placement for a fragment of velvet cloak on the jigsaw piece in her hand.

"I'm seeing him tomorrow anyway," Diana said.

"Don't get involved in mad stories about cafés that aren't there. You just go and offer him some kind words and comfort, a glimpse of the outside."

"I'm hoping he can help me with something."

"Oh?"

"Information on a former inmate he might have known. Marek Bogacki."

"You do get involved in some rum stuff, my girl."

"I try not to." Diana picked up a piece from the box and

resigned herself to an evening of Regency fun. "You can put Pride and Prejudice back on now, but is there any chance you could have the volume a bit lower?"

"Come again, love?" asked Bev, a hand cupped against her ear.

Diana shook her head.

CHAPTER THIRTY-ONE

ZAF WALKED along Piccadilly with something like trepidation. The evening social crowd was out in London and ahead were the lights of the Mayfair restaurant where he was to meet Alexsei for their six month anniversary meal.

He didn't know how he felt about it all. Up until the eviction bombshell, he'd felt nothing but love and contentment with Alexsei. Back then, the idea of anniversaries and 'special dinners' had felt grown up and comforting. Now, it felt superficial and silly, the kind of thing old people who'd given up on life indulged in.

And yet.... Zaf wasn't quite ready to throw in the towel with Alexsei. He might feel nothing but fury for Alexsei's dad, or at least the business empire and legal forces he hid behind, but Alexsei himself, even the thought of him, sparked romantic yearning and affection.

They had planned tonight's meal with some very cursory texts. Zaf had suggested that Alexsei choose somewhere, and as he entered the restaurant and looked around, he had the feeling Alexsei had decided to pull out all the stops. It felt expensive and formal.

Alexsei was already at the table. He stood to meet Zaf and leaned to kiss him. Zaf, torn between love and anger, let Alexsei peck his cheek.

"You like it here?" asked Alexsei.

"I sure do. It's quality," said Zaf.

As they prepared to dine, waiters swooped in to attend to them. They unfolded their napkins and laid them across their laps. Their drinks were topped up every time they took a sip. Alexsei knew how to ignore them, but Zaf felt flustered. He kept saying 'thank you' or 'sorry' for daring to exist.

The menu was madness. Truffle-infused Cauliflower Velouté, Charred Octopus Tostadas, Crispy Gochujang Broccoli Bites and Sesame-crusted Ahi Tuna Bowl. Zaf was sure those were all real words but struggled to understand what they meant.

"You're stopping with Diana's mum?" asked Alexsei.

Zaf looked up from his menu. "Bev, yes."

"How's it going?"

"Cramped. I'm looking at options."

Alexsei smiled. "Yeah?"

"Yeah."

"That's great news. You can come and move in with —"

"—erm, no. The option I was thinking about was the hostel next to the Guild of Tourism."

"Oh." Alexsei looked crestfallen. "I thought..."

He nodded and looked at his menu. Zaf tried to read his.

"What do you think a beetroot carpaccio might be?" said Zaf.

A smile. "Half the people who come into these places have

no more idea what all these stupid words mean than you or I do."

"This is the world you live in."

"Don't let superficial things confuse you. What do you think I'd rather be eating? Your scrambled eggs or – heck, what is this? – 'verjus-braised nopal ceviche'?"

Zaf laughed. "Yeah, but my scrambled eggs include the secret recipe."

"Barbecue sauce."

A waiter swooped in with a wooden platter on which three tiny crusts of bread had been artfully placed and took their order.

"I'm having what he's having," said Zaf when the waiter looked at him.

"And how would you like your main cooked, sir? Is it—"

"Exactly the same as what he's having."

The waiter departed and Zaf raised his glass. "Six months."

Alexsei chinked his glass against Zaf's. "Six months."

"Ups and downs. But possibly worth it."

"I sincerely hope so."

"Obviously, I'm just into you because you're fabulously wealthy."

"And I only showed an interest in you because you're a shamelessly crazy dancer and wear shirts that make my eyes hurt."

"Which shirts?"

Alexsei smiled. "That neon pink Hawaiian thing, for a start."

"Oh, that. It's beautiful. And ironic."

"Sears my eyeballs every time I look at it."

They laughed. They made each other laugh. Maybe that was what it all came down to.

Alexsei sighed. "I want us to back to the way we were. You cannot go live in a homeless hostel. You have a home with me, as soon as you want it."

"Has anything changed? Did you speak to your dad?"

"I told you. My father... I don't know how I could change his mind on this, I just don't."

Alexsei looked miserable. Zaf wanted to hug him, but this issue between them wasn't going anywhere.

He inhaled, and picked up the cologne Alexsei had worn on what he regarded as their first official date. It shook his resolve for a moment, the scent piercing through everything that had happened and transporting Zaf back to that magical evening.

The spell was broken by another waiter. "Finished with the bread?"

Zaf had nibbled half a tiny crust. "All done."

"You drifted away for a moment there," said Alexsei.

Zaf smiled. Alexsei read him so well. "What is it about scent that transports us so readily to another time and another place?"

"It is the way our brains are wired," said Alexsei.

"Just for a second, I felt as though it almost made me think of something important. Do you ever get that feeling?"

"I normally know when I am thinking of something important." He looked into Zaf's eyes. "See? I am doing it now."

Zaf smiled, and *almost* didn't notice when a waiter arrived with an elaborate scraper to collect crumbs from the tablecloth.

CHAPTER THIRTY-TWO

His Majesty's Prison Wandsworth was two buses and an underground and nearly an hour and a half from Diana's new home in Bromley-by-Bow. She'd never been one of those people who treated South London as some sort of alien country, but she rarely ventured this far south of the river.

She queued with other families and friends to enter the visitors' centre. After a series of searches and instructions, they were let into a large room that reminded her of a school hall. It was where the strange, emotional reunions between inmates and their loved ones took place.

She waited and soon Morris Walker came in, wearing the standard issue grey jogging bottoms and sweatshirt.

As always, he smiled and came over to her.

Morris had always been a sharp dresser. In his youth he'd been a ladies' man without a trace of irony. But now he was getting old and his good looks had given way to something more rugged. He would be over seventy by the time he was released.

She stood and he hugged her, fierce and warm.

"Sight for sore eyes, Diana, as always," he said as they sat down.

"How's things?" she asked.

"Somewhere between fair and awful."

It was a common enough reply. Diana waited for him to elaborate.

"I've been offered a move to the Elderly Prisoners Unit, and I'm considering taking them up on it."

"You're not old."

"Oh, this place makes you feel it quicker. Meanwhile, I'm coaching the boys ready for a performance."

Morris had found purpose volunteering in the Education Unit. He was masterminding a stage production of *Oliver!*. The musical about crooks and thieves seemed appropriate.

"That's wonderful," she said.

"A range of talents to work with."

He'd made a success of turning Diana and her friend Ariadne into backing singers for his group, ElectraBeat. If he could produce hit records with amateur singers and scrappy musicians, he could turn his hand to anything.

"You got my letter," he said.

"I did."

"I need you to go back to the café and see if those details check out."

"You think a woman with a Bichon Frisé called Marengo might still be there?"

"It was a Pomeranian, Diana, and you know it. I'm certain."

"I will," Diana said, then added, "It's closed now."

"The café?"

"It's gone. Changed hands. The greasy spoon is now a kebab shop. Not a huge change, but the owners have changed."

Even if the café had still been there, his alibi would be as leaky as a colander.

No one she or the police had asked had seen him at the café. His bank records had placed him miles away, emptying an account of defrauded cash.

"But look, anyway. Just look," he said.

There was a tight desperation in his voice.

Morris always put a brave front on prison life. But sometimes the darkness broke through, even if only in a few words.

But look anyway. Just look.

He had few links to the outside world. He'd never married or had children, and his family were distant. Diana might be his only real connection now.

"Of course I'll look," she said.

"Good. Good." His hands were on the table. She wanted to reach out and hold them.

Embraces were allowed at the start and end of visits, but not hand-holding. Too many illicit packages might be passed that way.

"How are you, Diana?"

She wasn't going to tell him about losing her home.

She simply wasn't.

"Things are fine. Zaf, the new tour guide, is doing his certification at the Guild of Tourism."

He smiled. "Still got 'Doctor not Mister' Blackthorn running that?"

"He's still there. I think Carolyn Desanti is the operational mastermind these days. They've also got this bloke Strandman. Estonian, although he's just come back from a decade in Africa or something. The place has seen better days but Zaf seems to be enjoying it."

"I've got one of that Desanti woman's books somewhere. Wanders around in the river muck, finding clay pipes."

"A very simplified version of things but yes. Mudlarking."

"Doubt there's much money in that."

"Oh, you know. Some of us enjoy what London has to offer, regardless of how much it pays. There was actually some nasty business up at the Guild – well, the hostel next door – that I thought you might be able to help me with."

"Oh?"

"Marek Bogacki."

For a moment, there was no recognition on Morris's face. Then his eyebrows rose. "Oh, Marek. There was a Marek in here. Polish chap. He was a rum one."

"Is that so?"

"A career criminal, not like yours truly. He was... what's the word? Unrepentant. He'd tell anyone who'd care to listen what he'd done. And if you believed half of what he said, he'd tell you he'd stolen the Crown Jewels and the Mona Lisa."

"I think he specialised in museums and galleries and the like."

"That's right. He was an odd chap. Didn't like being inside."

"I can't imagine many people do."

"No, I mean he generally disliked being inside places, houses in particular. He'd been in a house fire as a young man. Couldn't stand fire. What do they call it?"

"Pyrophobia?"

"That's the one. Couldn't work on the ovens in the kitchen. We were in the Education Unit, in the workshop. Someone was working on the sander or the lathe and sparks flew, and he all but hid in the corner."

"Really? He was living on the streets up until the day he died."

Morris's eyes widened. "He's dead?"

Diana nodded. "Found dead in the hostel. He'd been poisoned."

"Like carbon monoxide or something?"

"Not carbon monoxide. Literally poisoned."

"Bloody hell."

"Mmmm. So, I'm trying to work out who might have done it."

"You?"

"A woman needs her hobbies. So I'm asking around. I'm sure a man like Marek must've had enemies."

"I think, for the most part, us lot in here are our own worst enemies. No one hates us more than we hate ourselves."

"Oh, come, Morris."

"It's true. The world outside moves on and, apart from petty grievances in here, we don't have the freedom to make real enemies. I remember Marek Bogacki well. He'd tell his stories to anyone who'd listen because stories are sometimes all we have. But he was one of us."

"One of us?"

"The world has an endless supply of grey-haired old men. We cling to power and self-importance, but when that slips away, we become useless and all but invisible, Diana. And in the end, one fat old man is much like another."

"You should try being a woman some time," Diana said. "I can assure you it's the same, if not worse."

"I do not disagree for an instant. But we grey men, we're hollow kings. Empty shells. No one needs to make enemies of us. We're not worth the bother. Unless it's to punish us for the sins of our youth, no one has any reason to hate us."

She looked at him with affection.

Regardless of the crimes he'd been sentenced for, there was something in Morris Walker she couldn't help but love.

"My poor, poor hollow king."

"Yes. I might have accidentally waxed lyrical a bit there."

"Nearly poetic."

"I'm sorry to hear Marek is dead. He was an inoffensive old codger. Bit like me."

"Apart from the life of crime bit."

"Apart from that," Morris agreed.

CHAPTER THIRTY-THREE

Zaf went round to the hostel before classes the next day.

Arpinder didn't look happy as he pulled a room key from a drawer. "We have a room for you."

Zaf smiled, wondering what had changed. Had Diana had a word with someone?

He led Zaf upstairs to the floor where he'd rushed to help a few days ago. Even as Arpinder led him along the corridor, Zaf knew where they were going.

"This room, eh?" he said. It was Marek's old room.

Arpinder's smile faded. "I'm so sorry. You will not want to take this room. I will see what I can —"

"—It's fine," Zaf told him.

It didn't feel completely fine, but Zaf knew he shouldn't let squeamishness or superstition rule his life. If the only room available was the one recently vacated by a dead man, he was sure he could overcome his qualms.

Arpinder left him to settle in and Zaf sized up the space. He would go and fetch his bags from Bev's and make this little space his base of operations.

He opened the wardrobe and each of the drawers, mainly for something to do. The police would have removed everything of Marek's. As he closed the drawer he caught the ghost of a scent, just the faintest trace. He realised he remembered it from when he'd been here before. It was the smell that Marek had brought with him, presumably. The citrus notes had faded, leaving the woody part of the scent. It was a sophisticated scent for someone who was essentially a homeless criminal. In fact, it reminded Zaf slightly of Alexsei. It wasn't the same smell, but its understated opulence suggested it might be part of the same family of scents.

Zaf relaxed a little, trying to replace the image of Marek the sweat-drenched corpse with Marek the man who wore expensive cologne. If he was to inherit the man's living quarters then that would be a much more pleasing impression.

He supposed that Marek Bogacki had not always been that grubby homeless individual. At some point he'd have been a man with pride and affectations and things that brought him joy. Zaf had never experienced true homelessness, but had come startlingly close in his first months in London. He knew a life on the streets was only a hop, skip and a fall away for many people.

Every homeless person was two people: the person they had been and the person they had become. If Zaf was to remember Marek then he would try to picture the other man, the man he had been before.

Zaf went to classes feeling as if a weight had been lifted from his shoulders. If, by moving into the hostel, he could give Beverley and Diana a little bit of space back, he was sure it would make their lives a little easier. Of course, that left the gaping chasm of a problem that was him and Alexsei. How could he rebuild a connection with the man he loved while that man stood passively by and allowed his father's financial juggernaut to take Diana's home from her?

"Come on Zaf, jogging time!" yelled Jed, trotting past him. "It's not like you to be last!"

"Coming!"

Zaf rushed to catch up. The morning jog had become part of his routine, and he thought he might keep it up after the end of the course. The route was an extended circuit around the grounds of St Paul's, which was a very picturesque place to do some exercise.

"Out of the way!"

Zaf leapt aside as Josephine pelted past. He shook his head at her. She attacked the jog as if it was a race to the death every single day. Still, it probably worked better for her over-competitive nature.

Zaf had a long stride, so he caught up with Parvani on the way round and ran alongside her. "Morning!"

She nodded a greeting, but the jogging took its toll on her, and she didn't have the breath for an extended conversation.

Before long they were all changed and in the classroom, their faces flushed with the effort.

"Morning everyone," said Georg. "Today we will be thinking on our feet."

There were groans from several of the students, but Zaf wasn't intimidated by the idea. He relished the challenge.

"It will be the tour guide equivalent of improv," continued Georg. "You will all be given something to talk about for three minutes with no prep time. You can work alone or in groups. Sound good?"

Georg ignored the protests and had them all stand up. "Let's go over to the Cathedral for this. Plenty of material in there to talk about."

"Do we want to work in a group?" asked Parvani as they walked.

"Yeah! We could deliver the thing as a cheeky dance number," said Jed, throwing some dance moves as he made his way out of the room.

"Wait, no! Can I please ask you to be serious?" Parvani said. "Don't you want to win?"

Zaf smiled at her. "Don't you think we can win with the power of dance?" He added a few moves of his own by way of illustration. "Sometimes you need to startle your audience a little to get their attention."

"Fine. I think the two of you are saying that you will be in a group. I will do a solo effort. Some of us want to be taken seriously."

Zaf glanced over at Jed. He tried to ask a silent question with a look. Were they being unreasonable?

Jed's expression matched his shrug. No, they were not being unreasonable.

They walked through the Cathedral, Georg steering them towards the quieter parts.

"Who would like to go first?" he asked.

CHAPTER THIRTY-FOUR

Zaf looked up to see Parvani and Josephine both had their hands in the air.

"Right," said Georg. "Parvani first. Talk to us about the environmental footprint of St Paul's Cathedral."

"The what?" Parvani looked stricken. Josephine looked smug.

"Don't panic," said Georg. "Just talk to us and sound plausible."

Parvani looked horrified. "But what if I get things wrong?"

"I am not condoning making stuff up for clients, but I am asking you to fill three minutes of airtime for your fellow students. I want us to work towards being able to craft a fluent and engaging narrative at the drop of a hat. You can do this, Parvani."

Parvani nodded. "OK." She coughed lightly. "Across the Church of England, there is of course a commitment to reducing the environmental impact of its many properties."

Georg nodded. He made a rolling motion with his hands, encouraging her to go on.

"The aspiration is for St Paul's to be carbon neutral by the year twenty forty. There are a number of initiatives to move closer to that goal."

Zaf watched in admiration as Parvani pulled common-sense ideas out of the air. She talked about using low-energy lightbulbs and applying draughtproofing measures that were in keeping with the important aesthetic of the building. After three minutes were up, she was still talking. Nothing she'd said sounded far-fetched.

"Great job, Parvani," said Georg. "I've a feeling that if we fact-checked what you just said, it would be pretty accurate."

"Huh?" Parvani shrugged.

Zaf smiled: Parvani had just had a lesson in loosening up and winging it.

"Josephine next," said Georg. "Let's look at the altar cloth, shall we? Talk to us about that."

Everyone else followed Parvani's lead and embellished what they knew or what was obvious.

Then it was time for Zaf and Jed. They were in the crypt, and Georg asked them to talk about the mosaic flooring.

Zaf leaned in towards Jed. "Some of this was laid by women prisoners, that's all I know," he whispered.

Jed stepped forward onto the mosaic and started dancing. Zaf mirrored his movements. Once the two of them had established the moves, it seemed like they should start talking, so Zaf began.

"Mosaics have been used for many years to create a hard-wearing and decorative floor. What's interesting about this example is that it was laid, at least in part, by women from Woking Jail."

Zaf had already run out of things he knew about the floor,

and he'd barely filled twenty seconds. Jed was dancing with enthusiasm but didn't seem ready to take on the narrative.

Zaf's mind raced. He knew about art, so maybe he could fall back on the composition?

He cleared his throat. "As you can see, the quality of the work is variable across the floor. It would indicate that the people who laid it became more skilled as time went by. Who created the design though, and what can we discern from it? Well, you can see nautical elements, like these anchors. No coincidence, given that we are next to Nelson's tomb. Now let's take a moment to consider the use of black outlines. I would suggest that someone with greater skill or artistic vision laid out the bolder elements, mostly black, leaving the infill for those that followed on behind her. I like to think it demonstrates a quiet but efficient form of teamwork."

His mind raced ahead to the people who would be laying down the cement, and those who would apply the finish once the pieces were set in place. He was confident he could keep going. But Jed needed to step in.

"So, Jed!" he said. "Tell me what you think a day's work would look like for the team who made this?"

Jed's eyes widened. He hesitated, then started talking. "They would travel here daily from their quarters in the jail, which meant an early and uncomfortable ride for them. It's likely there would be ten or twelve of them working here at a time."

Once the three minutes were up and Jed had sketched out a daily routine for the women, they were able to stop dancing.

"Interesting approach," said Georg. "Do you feel the dancing was a useful addition?"

Zaf wasn't so sure.

"It's proven that physical movement can improve memory," said Jed.

Georg raised an eyebrow. "We all collect tools for our toolkit, but just make sure it doesn't confuse your audience."

As they all walked back to the classroom, Parvani caught up with Zaf and Jed. "See, I told you. He didn't approve of the dancing."

"That's not exactly what he said," replied Zaf. "It's good to mix things up when we're learning, surely?"

"Not if it loses us points on our assessment."

Ah, the assessment. Parvani was properly obsessed. Jed didn't seem bothered. Should Zaf be worrying more about it?

As they entered the Guild, Zaf remembered the peculiar little mission Diana had given him. The large clock above the Guild door was nearing noon, the two hands – brass or iron, he couldn't tell – close together on the twelve. If there was some problem with the clock or if someone had fiddled with it, it would explain how Diana had seen Marek Bogacki at a time when the man was supposed to be dead.

"I'll catch up with you in a minute," he told his friends and went to the stairs.

If there was any way of accessing the clock then it would have to be on the first floor. Maybe a little cupboard or a door or...

There it was! At the top of the stairs, in the wood-panelled wall, was a small door, no more than four feet high, almost flush with the panelling.

There was a handle and a keyhole but his luck was in: it was unlocked. Behind was a thin, dark and somewhat grimy cupboard, the bulk of which was taken up by a square metallic box with a door in it. Clock keys stuck out of it, the kind that looked very much like a cross between butterfly wings and human ears. And over everything, a thick layer of dust and grease that obscured any markings.

Whether Zaf could read it or not, it seemed possible that, from this position here, he would be able to make alterations to the clock.

As he fished in his pocket for a tissue or napkin to wipe away the greasy dust, he spotted a thin section that seemed cleaner than the rest. There was an inch-high line of cleared dirt with a thick thumb mark at the end.

"Huh."

"Have we got lost, Mr Williams?"

Zaf jumped up to see Dr Samuel Blackthorn behind him.

"Sorry. I was just..."

"Looking for your next lesson?"

There was sarcasm in Dr Blackthorn's voice, but an amused twinkle in his eye. The man's face was so dominated by his thick ruddy beard that it was hard to see past it. A beard could hide so many things.

"I... really..." said Zaf.

"Opening mysterious doors, eh?" said Blackthorn. "Sticking your nose in?"

"Um... I guess I'm just curious."

"An admirable quality in a tour guide, one might imagine." Blackthorn reached past him and closed the little cupboard door. "But remember what curiosity did?"

"Killed the cat?"

"Slaughtered it," rumbled Dr Blackthorn. "Best to keep our noses where they are meant to be. I'm sure I have a key for that little door somewhere."

He turned away and ambled along the corridor, glancing back once to check Zaf wasn't up to more mischief.

CHAPTER THIRTY-FIVE

Zaf was missing the depot, and the casual chats with Diana and Newton. So the next morning, with lessons not due to start until late morning, he decided to drop by.

"Zaf." Diana sat in the kitchen, flicking through a folder. Gus sat on the table opposite her, staring at her intently. "Can't you stay away from this place?" Diana asked him. "How's the course going?"

Zaf wanted to insist that everything was fine, but he couldn't lie to Diana. "It's been difficult in ways that I didn't expect."

Diana nodded. "You thought you'd sail through because you've got some really good experience and the right attitude."

"Well, yeah."

"I was the same. It's good to be challenged though, don't you think?"

Zaf pulled a face. "Maybe I'll think so once it's all over. Right now, it's pretty raw. I mean, what if I fail?"

"Oh, you'll be fine."

Did she mean that he'd definitely pass, or that he'd be OK even if he didn't? Zaf sighed. Either way, she was right.

Zaf sat down at the table. Gus nuzzled his face against his hand.

"You've missed me too, then? Seems oddly affectionate."

"He wants food," said Diana.

Zaf could hear clanking and manly groaning from outside in the warehouse. "Hasn't Newton fed him?"

"Our Gus is on a diet now."

"Is he?"

"Turns out he's been double-dipping, getting fed both here and somewhere else nearby. Our chunky boy is leading a double life and pretending to be two cats. Made himself a bit ill with the over-eating."

"Naughty boy." Zaf stroked the hungry cat's head.

"Newton is busy preparing the buses for their new owners," Diana said. Zaf heard the air-quotes around the word 'busy'.

"Not coping well?" he said.

More clanking and a groan that was more of a wail from outside was all the answer he needed.

"By the way, I checked on the Guild clock for you," Zaf said to Diana.

"You did? I thought you would ignore it. It was a mad little quest."

"I did think that. Obviously. But I looked anyway. The clock is quite accessible from a little cupboard on the first floor. In fact, it looks like someone else has been in there."

"Recently?"

He shrugged. "At some point in the last ten years. I've no idea. But if someone wanted to change the time, I think they could. I would have looked a little closer but Dr Blackthorn caught me snooping."

"Oh, dear. You didn't get into trouble?"

"No. I don't think so. He had a bit of a grumpy old bear vibe about him, though."

"It's the beard, you know. He's quite a softy. A finer academic of the history of London I have never met."

"I don't think I'm going to get called to the head teacher's office over it, anyway. I had the strangest thought yesterday. When I went to the hostel, the room they gave me was Marek Bogacki's."

"That was rather thoughtless."

Zaf shrugged. "Yeah, maybe. Anyway I realised that I could still smell, very faintly, the scent that he wore. It was stronger on the day that he died, but I caught the tiniest whiff and it reminded me."

"What sort of smell?"

"I'm not the greatest when it comes to describing scents. It's like wine, I imagine, you probably have to practise. I bet Alexsei would have the words to describe it but it was sort of citrussy with a woody smell underneath."

"Sounds sophisticated. So we're not talking about something he'd quickly doused himself in, to mask body odours."

"No, it was nice. Similar to one Alexsei wears, I'd swear."

"Unlikely to be cheap then, I guess."

"And that's the odd thing. I know we don't all have the same priorities, but the clothes he wore... they were cheap and worn like he was properly skint. How weird is it that you'd care about how you smelled more than how you looked?"

Diana looked away. "Indeed. Although sometimes, when things have gone wrong in our lives, we just need something that transports us to a better time and place. Scent will do that."

Zaf nodded. She probably had her own coping mechanisms for the horrible wrench she'd undergone.

He gave Gus's insistently demanding head a final stroke and turned on the kettle.

CHAPTER THIRTY-SIX

Diana had been delighted by Zaf's visit. The course would last another week and soon he would be back in the workplace, helping her scrape together some tours with fewer clients and, soon enough, even fewer buses. His youthful energy had brought a bit of positivity back to the downbeat atmosphere at Chartwell and Crouch.

She watched as he prepared to leave for his day's lessons.

"Is there an alumni dinner and dance this year?" she asked.

He frowned. "I think there's something on the calendar. I think it's optional."

"Very much not the case. The value of being an old girl or boy at the Guild of Tourism is the networking opportunity it represents. The people you study with and come across at the Guild may be your contacts in the industry for years to come."

"Really? OK then."

"And I will be invited too."

Comprehension dawned on his face. "A night on the town for Diana. OK. Let's do it. I'll find the date and let you know."

Once he had gone, she finished her tea slowly and stroked

Gus, who clearly wanted something more than mere affection, but had been thwarted by his diet. By the end of her cuppa, she had come to a decision.

She stepped from the little kitchen into the garage proper. Newton had his sleeves rolled up and the bonnet of one of his beloved Routemaster buses open. He was cleaning oily components with a terrible and vengeful passion. It was good to see him channelling his frustrations into something productive.

"I'm just going out," she told him.

Newton grunted.

"Going to investigate a café."

He said nothing. He was a deeply unhappy fellow at the moment.

Diana strode out along Chiltern Street and turned along Crawford Street to head west. The sun was high and very hot today and she put up her duck-headed brolly. It was only a twenty-minute walk to Sussex Gardens and the Best Western Hotel, but it was a walk best conducted in the shade.

Morris Walker's description of the café he had been in on the afternoon when he was allegedly withdrawing his ill-gotten gains from the bank was so freshly rendered in her mind that she felt as if she knew the place. Morris had spoken of the red seating and the glass counter and the slick-haired owner. He'd mentioned the coffee he'd drunk and the ham and mushroom bruschetta. He'd spoken more recently of the older woman, wearing furs or something similar, and a Pomeranian dog with the name Marengo. She felt she knew it intimately but knew she would, yet again, be unable to find it.

Sussex Gardens had an unusual and attractive layout. It was a true avenue. A central two lane road ran along it bordered by rows of trees and ornamental shrubs behind iron railings. Beyond these were narrower parallel roads that ran between the greenery and the large houses set far back from the road.

Many of these grand houses were businesses including the Best Western Hotel. Diana stood outside its door and, as if following cryptic treasure map clues given by Morris, set out to walk the block and explore all of the corners around which this mystery café might suddenly appear. Norfolk Place, Praed Street and London Street were the other sides of that block, plus the Norfolk Square Gardens in the middle of them all. There were many places on that journey, from an Italian restaurant to the Dickens Tavern to various McDonald's, KFCs and Subways on Praed Street. But in terms of cafés , there was only one place that came close. It now went under the name of *Knossos Café and Grill.*

Diana had been in before, and she went in again now. Ostensibly, it was a kebab shop. The menu sign above the counter listed various kebab options and chicken and chip deals. The lunchtime rush had not really started and she walked straight up to the unshaven man at the counter.

"Morning," she said.

"What can I get you?"

"I was wondering – Nikolaos, isn't it? – if you know if a woman who lives round here who owns a small Pomeranian dog?"

"What?"

"A Pomeranian. A fluffy little dog."

"You've lost your dog?"

"No, not me. I'm looking for the dog but it's not mine."

"This is a café. Chip shop."

"Yes," she agreed, "but I had been told she might have come in here."

"Today?"

"Not today. Some time ago. You don't know any women with Pomeranian dogs."

The man saw a way out here. "No. Sorry. Do you want something to eat?"

"Sorry. No."

She stepped outside onto the street. That had gone about as well as she had expected it to.

Should she post flyers through all the doors round here? *Do you own a Pomeranian dog? If so, please contact Diana Bakewell on etc, etc.* It was ridiculous. Reaching out via local social media might or might not be as effective.

Unsure what to do, she strolled over to Norfolk Square Gardens. There would be no answers there, but there was a statue of Paddington Bear to say hello to and a place where she might sit and contemplate the conundrum of Morris's missing café.

As she sat on a bench, she considered who else might have some insight into Morris's thinking and help her determine if he was lying, confused or downright deluded. Like Newton Crombie, she had worked for Morris for several years at Chartwell and Crouch. Before that she had got to know him through the music industry. She had provided backing vocals for Morris's ElectraBeat pop group. Morris had sung, with Diana and Ariadne Webb performing backing vocals. Ken Ferrari had been a wizard on the keyboards. Pascal Palmer had provided drums but, more importantly, had co-produced every record alongside Morris.

For a time, the five of them had been inseparable. They'd recorded, they'd toured. That had been the start of Ariadne and Pascal's twenty-year relationship. After the bust ups and the shouting matches and the silent treatment that marked the breakup of the band, Diana had been a willing shoulder for Pascal to cry on when he and Ariadne fell apart.

Life was a long, messy and intricate thing. People, like relationships, were complicated. Diana needed help to understand the wild and impossible goose chase Morris had set her on.

She and Ariadne were on speaking terms, but the words spoken were rarely nice. Ken Ferrari, the last she'd heard, had taken his fondness for alternative living and kooky mysticism to its natural end and was off drifting from one spiritual retreat to another. Pascal... At least Pascal Palmer was still rational, friendly and capable of providing moments of wisdom.

Diana put her umbrella down beside the bench, took out her phone and composed a message to Pascal.

CHAPTER THIRTY-SEVEN

ZAF HAD SAT through another day of lectures at the Guild of Tourism. Dr Blackthorn had bored them all with Roman-era Londinium and Georg Strandman had made them answer quickfire questions and complaints.

After saying goodbye to Jed, Zaf and Parvani headed to their rooms at the hostel, parting ways at the first floor. He was putting his key in the lock when Georg appeared, his bulky frame filling the corridor.

"Ah, roommates," he said. His European accent made it sound like roommates were something to be relished.

Zaf stepped back. "Just moved in. Had a..."

The teacher nodded. "You are not from here originally."

Zaf had spent his life dealing with people seeing his skin colour and asking where he was from 'originally'. It was code for 'you're not British'. As though Britishness belonged to only one type of person.

But George Strandman was Estonian. If either of them was the stranger here, it wasn't Zaf.

"The accent?" Zaf hazarded. "I'm from Birmingham. You know it?"

Georg nodded. "All the canals. And Aston Villa."

"Among other football clubs. You've been in Africa recently, right?"

"Egypt."

"What's that like?"

"Cairo is beautiful. The people are friendly." He moved past Zaf and to his own door. "I came back with a wallet stuffed full of Egyptian money. All colours. I had maybe three thousand Egyptian pounds."

Zaf's eyes widened. "Wow."

"Went to change it last week. Eighty quid, it was worth."

"I never realised how expensive the UK is until I moved to London."

Georg shook his head. "It's shocking." He slapped his door frame. "Still, we have roofs over our heads and food to eat. We should be grateful for such things."

He opened his door and went inside. Zaf did the same.

A roof over his head and food to eat. That was about all Zaf could say for his current situation. He dropped his bag and notebook onto the chest of drawers that served as his desk. The notebook hit the back wall and dropped down the back.

"Damn it." Zaf bent to retrieve it.

The chest of drawers was flush with the floor, and there was no gap to reach into. He rocked the drawers forward, widening the gap. At the bottom he found dust and a collection of lost items.

Zaf pulled out his notebook. And a slim paperback curled around a cylindrical, amber-coloured object. He freed them and let the chest of drawers sit flat again.

The object was a candle, four inches tall and an inch thick.

It was new, but the wick was dark and burned. He sniffed it. That woody, fruity, smoky smell.

He'd noted the scent in the room before.

"Well." Satisfied with the discovery, he turned to his books.

And saw the cover of the book he'd found. It was old, with creases and rough edges as if it had been read many times. The title was *The Ludgate Candlesticks: a Deep Dive*. The author: Georg Strandman.

This book had been here before him. A book written by his roommate. This book had been here when this room had been occupied by Marek Bogacki.

It had been brought here by Marek.

All but wrapped around the candle that had given its scent to the room on the night Marek died.

Zaf stared at the book, his heart racing. He knew. Something, at least.

Marek had come here to rob the Cathedral.

CHAPTER THIRTY-EIGHT

ZAF, Jed and Parvani sat at the back of the lecture theatre, notebooks open and pens poised. The rest of the students were already packing up, keen to head to the pub in the late afternoon sunshine.

It had been a long day spent learning about London's most famous river. Carolyn Desanti's lecture had covered the formalities, legal requirements and health and safety aspects of working on the Thames. She'd shown them a list of organisations they'd need to deal with if they wanted to do anything more complicated than take a selfie on a bridge.

As they'd filed out, Jed whispered to Zaf, "The MPU. That's the police people, right? But here I've put PLA in my notes. It's not the Palestine Liberation Army, is it?"

Zaf nodded. "Port of London Authority."

Parvani was still in her seat, scribbling furiously. She always took more notes than anyone else.

Zaf looked at her notebook. "Lessons are over."

"Nearly there." She put a final full stop on her work. "I do like Carolyn's lectures. She actually teaches us things."

"As opposed to...?"

"Georg's method. Haven't you noticed?"

Zaf frowned. Whatever it was, he hadn't noticed.

"His lessons are very practical," he said.

"Pretend tour activities, problem solving. But what about learning the history of this city or the things we need to know, legally speaking, to be tour guides?"

"Did you not hear the marvellous speech about the crypt mosaics I gave earlier?"

"But that was you. He makes us do all the work ourselves."

"It's the Socratic teaching method," said Jed.

Zaf gave him a look.

"Possibly," Jed admitted. "I don't actually know what that means."

"And besides, you're wrong about lessons being over." Parvani pulled her folder towards her and tapped the week's schedule. "Tonight's the 'practice drill' activity in the crypt. We've only got half an hour's break before it starts."

"More work." Jed sighed.

"At least it's Dr Blackthorn leading it. We might actually learn something."

Zaf, Jed and Parvani stood in a team huddle, peering down the spiral stairs to the entrance of the crypt.

"Now," Parvani said. "Don't be fooled by the fact that this is called a practice drill. This counts towards our assessment."

"How are we supposed to prepare if we don't even know what it is?" Jed shifted from foot to foot.

"By resolving to work effectively as a team," Parvani replied. "Yeah?"

They nodded.

"We're good then. Let's go."

They had exclusive use of St Paul's crypt for the evening,

and the space echoed as they crossed it. Josephine's group were waiting at the entrance, shifting from foot to foot as if they needed the loo.

"Welcome." Dr Blackthorn was waiting for them by the spiral stairs, the only part not taken up by scaffolding. "Down you go. I'll come and meet you in a moment when we're all inside."

He herded them into the shadowy crypt where the actors who'd accompanied them to Oxford Street were waiting. The big man, Pete, stood next to a pile of emergency blankets, rubbing his hands like he was cold.

"Hello again." Terry, the actor from their Disney Store challenge, stretched out, readying himself.

Dr Blackthorn led the students past the actors to where the marble columns faded into the darkness. "This event is a practice drill for the kind of situation that we all hope will never arise. You'll simulate a disaster and do what you can to ensure the safety of your tour group. The group will, of course, be portrayed by our actors. You'll recognise some faces from our recent excursion."

There were nods from the students and smiles from the actors.

"I have the scenario here." Blackthorn patted his jacket pocket, where Zaf assumed the script for the evening's 'activity' was kept. "I'll read it out in a moment. There will also be a wildcard at the end of the exercise. This will be a complicating factor, the kind of extra information that can often arrive late in a real life scenario. It will play into the results and the judging."

Zaf, Jed and Parvani were in a tight huddle, waiting to hear what disaster they would be dealing with.

"I've set up your scenarios in different parts of the crypt, to avoid any distraction by the activities of your counterparts."

"More like so they can't copy us," Parvani muttered.

"If you're ready." Blackthorn cleared his throat. "The actors have been briefed, so they'll go to their stations. Teams, your scenario is this: The building is a village hall in a rural location about two hours' drive from London. A utilities helicopter has crashed into the roof of the building. The pilot and a number of other casualties are on site. You have thirty minutes to determine the most effective ways to help. There's a working phone which you can use to simulate any calls you'd care to make. To your areas!"

Zaf, Jed and Parvani were ushered to their side of the crypt, near the case that held the copy of Christopher Wren's death mask.

"I can't see the point," Jed said. "I mean, what are the chances of—"

"Shush," said Parvani. "If we can deal with this, then we can cope with anything. Let's show them what we can do, shall we?"

Zaf and Jed exchanged glances.

"Fair enough," said Zaf. He patted the cabinet. "Wish us luck, Christopher."

The actors had spread themselves around the floor and the furniture as if they'd been flung there by unseen forces. Terry Rolls groaned and clutched his leg. "Lost control of the damned chopper, didn't I?"

Zaf said, "What first?"

"Zaf, will you call for help?" Parvani pulled her hair back into a ponytail, all business-like. "Jed and I will triage the patients."

Zaf went over to the phone. "On it."

"Have we made sure the area's safe first?" Jed asked.

"It looks safe to me." Parvani knelt next to the unconscious actors, checking their pulses. "Let's check out the unconscious ones first."

By the time the operator, who was being played by yet another actor, had captured the basic details from Zaf, the other two had finished their assessment. "We've got two unconscious, three conscious but suspected broken limbs, and two walking wounded," Parvani said.

"The operator wants me to stay on the line and tell them about each of the casualties." Zaf pointed at the phone. "Come over here and we can do this one first."

Parvani looked around the room. The casualties were dotted around a wide area. "You know what? Let's get as many of these casualties as we can into the area where Zaf is. It will help us to keep a better eye on them all as well as update the emergency services. Like a field hospital, yeah?"

Jed ushered some of the more mobile actors over to stand by Zaf. "Walking wounded, yeah? We surely shouldn't move the others though?"

"We're spread too thinly. I think we should move everyone who's conscious and able to move themselves." Parvani knelt next to Zaf. "Jed, you encourage them to move. Zaf, I will talk you through the unconscious ones. Let's start with this one. What questions does the operator have?"

Zaf relayed information back and forth between Parvani and the operator, while Jed shepherded the other casualties to assemble at his feet. It felt weird to be standing, so Zaf crouched down and offered comforting smiles to the actors, and a pat on the arm here and there.

There was the sound of sirens and Dr Blackthorn walked forward, signalling the end of the session. "The emergency services are here to take over. Thank you, ladies and gentlemen who are playing our casualties. Would you mind staying where you are while we reflect upon the outcomes?"

CHAPTER THIRTY-NINE

BLACKTHORN FLICKED THROUGH HIS NOTES.

"Now." He sighed. "There was an unfortunate oversight by this group, which you *almost* picked up. Do you see that one of your unconscious patients is lying on top of a thick cable? If you look closely, you'll see that it is clearly labelled as a *live* high voltage power cable. There is also a hosepipe over there which has been flooding the entire floor with water. So anyone in contact with the floor has been electrocuted, and is now dead." He surveyed the group. "That's all of you and every single casualty too."

Parvani's mouth fell open. Jed and Zaf looked at each other in horror. Zaf wanted to argue that the hose didn't look like it was connected to a water supply, but in truth he hadn't even seen it. None of them had.

"Let's hope that this has been a valuable learning experience for you all," said Georg. "Casualties, you can get up now."

"Thank goodness!" said Terry Rolls, stretching to his full height and then touching his toes before waggling his hands and feet. "This floor's chilly, even without the electricity and water."

Zaf stole a glance at Blackthorn's marking sheet and saw that Josephine's group had scored nine points compared with the big fat zero that they'd gained. He sighed and went over to comfort Parvani, who looked crumpled and defeated. Jed joined them.

"Come on, it's not the end of the world," said Jed.

"It was you that suggested checking the area was safe, though. And me that ignored you," wailed Parvani. "We should have done a safety scan. I let us all down. One of you needs to take over as team leader."

"Absolutely not," said Zaf. "You're the right person for this. If I know anything about you at all I guarantee that for as long as you live you'll never make that mistake again. I would happily put my life in your hands, Parvani."

"Me too," said Jed.

She attempted a watery smile. "We failed at teamwork though. It's like the two of you are a team and then there's me."

Zaf laid a hand on Parvani's. "I'm sorry. I'm not sure we even noticed what we were doing. Now you've pointed it out we'll try harder." He looked at Jed, who nodded.

Teas and coffees were served in the crypt for everyone. Zaf thought it was a great venue for a social gathering. Terry Rolls seemed to know all of the other actors, and was at the centre of their little gathering, talking about a job he'd done on a cruise ship, playing a victim at a murder mystery dinner.

"I had to lie on the floor like this, but with the smell of the most delicious food all around me. Honestly, can you imagine? It took all my resolve to stay in character, and I was ravenous by the time the case was solved. Scent can affect us in ways we don't expect."

"I've been doing some sums," said Parvani, approaching Zaf. "We're quite a bit behind on the marks so far, but because the final project is worth such a big part of the total, we could still come first."

"What is the final project?" asked Zaf.

"We'll find out in the next few days," she told him, "but it should be some sort of original idea we come up with as a group."

"Great," said Jed. "We can do that."

"But we need to do *really* well," said Parvani. "We can't just win, we need to completely kill it."

Parvani and Jed turned towards the stairs leading up out of the crypt.

Zaf hesitated. "I just want to take another look at the Ludgate Candlesticks."

Jed wrinkled his nose. "Doing some extra learning on the side?"

Zaf pulled the folded book from his back pocket. "I found this book, written by Georg, our Georg. It was in Marek's room."

"You mean your room," said Parvani.

Zaf led them to the cabinet holding the two ornate candlesticks. "These things are so intricate, so very valuable. Look." He opened the book and gestured at the carvings. "The stem is carved with scenes that show one guy living in wealth and another in poverty. That dude's got these luxurious robes on and is surrounded by luxury, while this other guy's got threadbare clothing and is lying outside this gate. He's overlooked and forgotten."

"It's the Rich Man and Lazarus," said Parvani.

"The what?" said Jed.

"It's a parable," she said.

"She's right," said Zaf. He looked at the detailed carving in his book and compared it to the real thing. "This other candlestick shows the afterlife consequences of their earthly choices. The Rich Man is in hell, surrounded by flames. Meanwhile, that guy's in a sort of heaven of tranquillity and fulfilment."

He looked closely at the carving on the poor Lazarus's face, and the one in the book. Maybe it was the light down here in the crypt, but one had quite a different face and expression to the other. He took out his phone and fired off a couple of photos.

"Are you three staying down here all night?" Dr Blackthorn called to them. "Security will want to have words."

Zaf considered the case the candlesticks stood in. It was locked, of course. How easy would it be for a thief to force it open? And what alarms would be triggered if they did?

CHAPTER FORTY

Zaf hadn't reckoned on maths being part of his course, but of course it was. Maths was everywhere.

Parvani loved the maths sessions. Making columns of numbers do her bidding seemed to satisfy her passion for organising the world.

During a break, Zaf said, "It's not that I dislike maths. It definitely has a place."

"The calculating part can be done on a phone, anyway," Jed replied.

"That last session about discounts, tips and kickbacks was a bit dry. Surely life's not like that?"

"It's important," Jed said. "It's the one-two-three rule my dad taught me."

Zaf raised an eyebrow. "My old man never taught me no rule."

"He wasn't a tour guide." Jed grinned. "He used to run a window cleaning business. It's like a guide for not losing money. Stick to it."

"Stick to what?"

Jed nodded. "One-two-three. The first is discounts, so that's number one." He held up a finger. "If you get asked for a discount then you might want to say yes, but it should never be more than ten per cent."

"Right."

"Then tips. If someone wants to offer a tip, either to us or someone else we encounter, it should always be twenty per cent, right?" He held up two fingers.

Zaf considered. "I got given these crazy tips by this woman on a tour once. It was like she was trying to buy me."

Jed laughed. "You could tell her the company has a policy of capping tips at twenty per cent, even if they don't. It stops things getting weird."

Zaf nodded. It was a good idea.

"Number three is kickbacks. If someone has created a load more business for someone else, maybe there's a kickback due. That might go up to thirty per cent."

"Dodgy."

"No!" Parvani frowned. "It's part of the business model when you design a new tour. You wouldn't call it a kickback, even if it is. You'd call it a loyalty bonus or something."

Zaf reeled. Had he been naive to think the world worked in any other way?

Later, there was a test on the maths concepts they'd covered. The scenarios were about how much money should change hands in different circumstances on a tour.

Zaf came out of the test and gave Jed a slap on the shoulder. "I didn't struggle for a second with any of those questions, because I kept your one-two-three rule in my head."

Jed grinned. "Simples."

"This feels like proper teamwork," Parvani said. "Great work everyone."

Jed led them to a halt in the corridor. "Now, what are we all going to wear to the big alumni dinner?"

"Clothes?" Parvani shrugged. "I was just going to wear...you know." She waved a hand up and down over her practical trousers and top.

Zaf and Jed exchanged a look.

"What?" Parvani bit her bottom lip. "You two know something you're not telling me."

Zaf linked his arm with Parvani's and Jed took her other side. "I think we've both come to the same conclusion without having to discuss it," Zaf told her. "How would you like your two new gay BFFs to help you with your outfit?"

Parvani gave a nervous laugh. "I can't go clothes shopping."

"We probably don't need to buy stuff. Please Parvani, pleeease." Jed batted his eyelashes.

"Fine," huffed Parvani. "Let's do it."

CHAPTER FORTY-ONE

DIANA HAD BEEN LOOKING FORWARD to the alumni dinner, even if it was simply a chance to spend the evening with people doing something other than completing jigsaws and watching The Chase. Both were mental pursuits that exercised the brain but, day-in, day-out, they were somehow deadening to the senses.

That evening, the main hall of the Guild of Tourism had been elegantly transformed for the annual alumni dinner in an attempt to marry historical grandeur with contemporary sophistication. Strings of soft fairy lights adorned the oak panelling, around set tables dressed in crisp white linen. Floral centrepieces and candelabras had been placed on each table and a jazz band played soft music in one corner.

Diana caught sight of Carolyn Desanti as she entered the room and, snagging a glass of wine from a passing waiter, went over to greet her. When she got there and saw that Carolyn was deep in conversation with Ariadne Webb she was less pleased. She had nursed a forlorn hope that Ariadne might have declined the invitation for some reason, but there she was.

"Hi both!" said Diana, determined to enjoy herself.

"Ah, Diana," said Ariadne. Her face was a mask of insincere sorrow. "Ernie told me that you'd lost your splendid flat. How are you coping?"

Diana hadn't expected Ariadne to know about that, but of course she did. She forced a smile, even though each new reminder felt like a knife to her heart. "I am coping well, thank you, Ariadne. It's surprising what we can tolerate if we put our minds to it."

"Of course, that used to be my flat, if I recall correctly," said Ariadne, addressing her comment mostly to Carolyn, as if it were important their former teacher should know such things.

"This is the one you rented off a Beatle?" said Carolyn.

"George was a wonderful supporter of people wishing to enter the arts," said Ariadne. "Rented it out to me—"

"To us," put in Diana.

"– but initially to me," said Ariadne, "oh, over forty years ago. And now Diana has lost it."

Carolyn twirled her drink thoughtfully and looked across the crowded room. "Life has these horrid ways of throwing curve balls at you."

Across the way, Diana could see Zaf talking animatedly with his fellow students and the barrel-chested and bearded lecturer, Georg Strandman. It was a formal dinner event, and apparently Zaf had decided to celebrate by wearing a bold floral shirt with his jacket. Still, he was better dressed than Strandman, who appeared to have been hard pressed to rustle up a suit of any sort.

"I think none of us are the people we thought we'd be when were last all together, doing your training," said Carolyn with a sigh.

"You were a celebrated mudlarker even then," Diana observed.

"A celebrity, indeed. Riding high. A supportive husband at my side. The husband is definitely gone and the career with it too, I think."

"Oh, husbands are totally over-rated," said Ariadne. "I gave my feller the heave-ho two decades ago and I've never looked back. Although I believe Diana here still sniffs round him from time to time."

"Pascal and I remain on cordial terms," said Diana. Seeking fresh and less miserable conversation, she turned to Carolyn. "Carolyn, any interesting mudlarking finds since I saw you last?"

Carolyn smiled. "Everything on the foreshore is interesting in its own way. Someone found a Roman beaker intact in the mud last week. It's amazing when things like that are preserved with relatively little damage."

"Was it a poppy beaker?" asked Ariadne.

"As a matter of fact it was." Carolyn looked surprised that Ariadne would know about such things.

"Made at the Roman pottery that existed at Highgate Wood," said Ariadne with a nod. "Called a poppy beaker because it was shaped like the seed head of a poppy. I bet whoever found that was delighted."

"Oh yes," said Carolyn.

Diana knew a lot about the history of London, but Ariadne had a habit of pulling nuggets like this out of nowhere. There was a time when it would have delighted Diana, because a conversation with Ariadne could never flag. Now, though, she felt that Ariadne used it to prove over and over again that she was Diana's superior.

"We can sit over here," said Carolyn when it was time for food to be served.

There was no head table at this dinner event but the layout suggested subtly that this particular long table was for the Guild lecturers and a selection of old boys and girls.

Diana waved to Zaf and Ariadne waved to Jed as they saw them sitting in their own group.

"How's your lad getting on?" asked Ariadne.

"Very well, I think," said Diana.

"Some tensions in their group I believe. I do hope they can resolve them."

Diana silently fumed. How was it that Ariadne had managed to extract such detail from Jed? She was sure that whatever problems Zaf might be having, he would keep them to himself as long as he felt he was on top of them, but once again, Ariadne had said something that irked Diana.

Diana sat down between Ariadne and the lecturer, Strandman.

"Mr Strandman," she said, offering him her hand, "I don't think we've ever been formally introduced."

Strandman struggled to focus on her. He was a big man and there was a certain clumsiness about him. He shook her hand.

"Georg, please. Everyone calls me that."

"My work colleague, Zaf, speaks highly of you. You are, I believe, the 'fun' teacher."

"I heard that," said Carolyn on the other side of Ariadne.

Dr Samuel Blackthorn made a rumbling sound as though he had intended to say the very same thing.

"That's lovely to hear," Georg said. His accent wasn't as light and lilting as Diana had expected, with him being Estonian. Or maybe she'd misheard Carolyn?

Servers brought the starter, a terrine on a bed of watercress.

Georg turned his plate around in front of him.

"Wondering if it's made from leftovers?" Diana enquired with a smile.

In the flickering candlelight of the candelabras, Georg looked queasy. She hoped he wasn't unwell.

"Wondering if it has been poisoned, perhaps," quipped Ariadne.

"Ariadne, please," said Dr Blackthorn.

"Just making a joke. It's not poisoned, is it?"

"I think that matter has been all but cleared up," said Carolyn. "A man is dead, and that is a sad business. Lack of proper organisation and too many people coming in and out of that place next door possibly at the root of it all."

A man had been deliberately poisoned. Diana couldn't see how that could be blamed on sloppy bureaucracy.

"I've been intrigued by the death of that poor man next door," she said. Both Carolyn and Georg gave a polite nod, offering no thoughts.

"Another homeless statistic," said Dr Blackthorn. "Par for the course, sadly."

"You're both drawn to that sort of thing, aren't you?" Ariadne said to Diana.

"That sort of thing?"

"Death. Is it the drama, would you say?"

"Drama." Diana turned the word over in her mind. "If you were to re-phrase that to 'the human impact of shattering events' then yes, Zaf and I are very drawn to that sort of thing. We care about people."

"Diana, the people person," chuckled Ariadne. "So what theories do you have about the death of that man, Diana?"

"Do we have to?" said Carolyn.

"His name was Marek Bogacki," said Diana. *Not that man.*

"You knew him?" asked Blackthorn.

"Not at all. By all accounts, he was a man with a criminal past. He was poisoned, though, and nobody deserves that, even if they have a fondness for stealing religious artifacts."

"It's not as if it's contagious, is it?" Georg had pushed himself back from the table as if he needed air.

"Have the police found any reason that a person would want to kill Marek?" asked Blackthorn.

"If they have, then they have not shared it with me."

"What? Don't they keep you updated at all times?" asked Ariadne.

Diana laughed. "Sadly, they don't."

"They could save us all a lot of time if they just told you everything."

Diana pursed her lips. Ariadne was being snippy with her, but she was absolutely right.

The main course was served: slices of roast pork with vegetables. Enormous jugs of gravy were set upon the table. Georg reached out to take one, then pulled back as though thinking better of it.

Carolyn ate lightly and after a few minutes, declared reluctantly, "Time for a speech, I guess."

"It is required," said Blackthorn.

"But remember, all the best speeches are short," said Ariadne.

As Carolyn moved towards the stage, Blackthorn leaned towards Ariadne and Diana. "I think we should keep talk of poisonings to a minimum, don't you?"

"Sorry if it was tactless of us," said Diana.

"Least said, soonest mended." Blackthorn's eyes flashed darkly beneath his brows. The candlelight lent a savage aspect to his face. "If you ask me, we shouldn't be having homeless people in the hostel any more."

"No?" said Diana.

"If we are to raise our profile and fill our coffers then we should offer as many spaces as possible to students and visitors. This is St Paul's, for goodness sake."

"St Paul's not a place for the poor and needy, eh?" Georg said, the first time he'd spoken in a while. "Not a place for charity?"

"Oh, you know what I mean, Georg." Blackthorn's tone was testy.

Carolyn took to the stage. The little jazz band fell quiet and a microphone was presented to her. Carolyn knew how to work a crowd. She'd done enough book signings and TV appearances on her mudlarking specialism. From her "Good evening, everyone, I hope you're enjoying your meal," through to her final, "the Guild lives or dies on the support of its wonderful alumni," she managed to be rousing, personable and more than a little pleading for donations, all within the space of five minutes.

She departed the stage, the jazz band set up with some livelier tunes and the dessert course was brought out.

"I think I will skip pudding," said Georg, pushing his chair back further to stand. His face was covered with a sheen of sweat. He seemed positively unwell.

"It was nice to meet you," said Diana, but he was already moving quickly away, as if he hadn't even heard her.

Hands touched Diana's shoulder and she jumped. It was Zaf.

"You gave me a shock!"

"Sorry." He bent to whisper in her ear. "I need to talk to you."

She tensed. "Everything all right?"

"I have a piece of the mystery and it doesn't make sense."

He let go of her shoulders and moved away towards a quieter, darker corner of the room, with a single backward glance inviting her to follow.

"Excuse me a moment," she said to the rest of the table and went after Zaf.

CHAPTER FORTY-TWO

ZAF WATCHED Diana follow him into the Guild of Tourism lobby. "I didn't mean to drag you away from your dinner."

"Oh, you probably just saved everyone from me and Ariadne sniping at one another."

He beckoned her over. "There's this thing I wanted to show you."

"What is it?"

He pulled the Ludgate Candlesticks book and the candle stub from his inside jacket pocket. "I found this in my room."

She looked at each item. "A book."

"It had fallen down the back of the chest of drawers along with the candle. The candle was the smell I could smell before. And it was what I smelled when we... found him that morning." He held out the book. "Marek Bogacki had a book which included information on the valuable candlesticks inside the Cathedral."

"Written by Georg Strandman."

"I know. Coincidence or what?"

"It is."

"But, look, tell me I'm going mad." He flicked through the book to the page with the photo illustration of the carvings. "See this man here."

"Yes."

He held out his phone and showed her the picture he'd taken. "Is this the same or is it different? Look at his face. Look at his expression."

Diana frowned. "They're not the same. I don't know if it's the light..."

"That's what I thought."

"But that one there in your photo. It looks a bit squashed. Like someone has bashed it in."

"And the one in the book doesn't look like it's been bashed."

"No."

Zaf stepped back, thinking. "What can that mean?"

"Someone has damaged the candlesticks?" she suggested.

"Or the candlesticks in the book are not the same as the ones currently in the Cathedral."

"How could that come about?"

"Maybe they're fakes?" Zaf suggested. "Someone swapped them out? Marek Bogacki had this book..."

"The notorious thief swaps fakes for the real thing? Sounds like a lot of effort." She twitched her nose. "Marek Bogacki strikes me as a man with an enthusiasm for theft rather than one who was devoted to convoluted plans."

"But if the candlesticks in there are fakes then he must have stolen the priceless originals."

Diana tapped the edge of the book. "It sounds like Mr Strandman is the expert to ask."

Zaf looked around. "He left the dinner rather early, didn't he?"

Diana nodded. "He seemed positively unwell. He was sweating like he had a fever."

"Sweating...?" A fear gripped Zaf. "Organophosphate poisoning. It only takes a small quantity."

"Who'd want to poison Georg?"

"We don't know the murderer's motives." He ran to the exit. "Where did he go?"

The answer was obvious. If he was ill, he'd have gone back to his rooms. The hostel.

Zaf burst into the lobby, slamming the door wide. He hurried to the stairs. Diana followed, and the receptionist Arpinder called out, "No guests in rooms! No guests in rooms!"

Zaf took the stairs three at a time, skidded on the first floor corridor and ran to Georg's room. He hammered on the door. "Georg! Sir! Are you alright?"

There was no sound from within. He strained to hear breathing or groaning. Nothing. He hammered again. "Georg! Georg! Wake up!"

Zaf put his ear to the door and rattled the handle. The door was locked. He tried a shoulder barge. The solid door frame told him he wasn't built for breaking down doors.

"Damn!" He ran back down.

Diana was on the last flight of stairs, following him. "What's happening?"

There was no time to stop. Zaf called back as he sped past her.

"I think he could already be dead."

CHAPTER FORTY-THREE

Zaf had to haul the receptionist up by the arm. Flustered explanations about illness and poisoning and fake candlesticks didn't help one bit.

Eventually, Zaf had him on the first floor and was waving at the door.

"Go on, go on! Get it open!"

Arpinder had a master keycard in his hand. "He might just be sleeping."

"You want to take that chance?"

Diana watched silently as Zaf urged the receptionist on. Arpinder swiped, and with a call of "We're coming in!" thrust the door open. The room was in darkness. Zaf reached for the light switch. His hand brushed something papery on the wall which fell before he located the switch.

Clothes lay scattered untidily around the room. The chest of drawers was cluttered with a mess of toiletries. The bed was unmade. But there was no Georg Strandman.

Zaf was about to step forward to check the bathroom when he heard a voice.

"What is going on here?"

Zaf whirled.

Georg Strandman stood in the corridor, still in his dinner attire. His tie had been loosened and the top three buttons undone.

"I'm sorry," said Zaf. "I… I thought you were dead."

The big man smiled. "Dead?"

"We might have jumped to some conclusions," said Diana.

"I just needed some air," said Georg. "Lots of people around me, I… I'm fine."

Diana bent to pick something up. The thing Zaf had dislodged from the wall had been a photograph. It was an old colour photo, faded. Two brown-haired women, possibly sisters, possibly friends, crowded together to fit into the frame.

Diana flipped it over.

"Anna and Krystyna," she read.

Georg stepped forward and took it from her.

"Your concern for my safety is admirable," he said. "But seriously, friends, I am fine."

Arpinder looked sheepish and gestured at Diana and Zaf. "It was their idea. They sounded so certain."

"Better to be too cautious, eh?" said Georg, and slid past the little group to his door. "But now I must rest."

Inside, he shut the door in their faces.

"Is this some sort of prank?" said Arpinder.

"Sometimes our imagination gets the better of us," said Diana.

Arpinder was unimpressed. Zaf and Diana left as quickly as they could.

"Damn it," said Zaf. "I forgot to ask Georg about the candlesticks."

"Another time, perhaps."

Diana looked to the Guild building. "Return to the dinner?"

"I think there'll be dancing."

Diana put her arm through Zaf's. "How are things with you and Alexsei?"

He pulled a face. "On hiatus, I think. The anniversary dinner was lovely but... but how do we move forward while you're being made to suffer?"

"I'm not suffering. Living with Mum is an experience, but I just get out as often as possible. I've got lunch with Pascal later this week."

Zaf nodded. Pascal was an old friend of Diana's and a professional restaurant critic.

"Well, I guess he'll be taking you somewhere nice then."

They headed back into the Guild of Tourism together.

CHAPTER FORTY-FOUR

Diana sat with her mum the next morning as they both ate breakfast at the foldout table.

"How about I cook for us both tonight?"

"You don't need to do that, love. I'm at home all day so it's no bother for me to pop something on."

"I'd like to, though."

What she'd really like, she thought, was a bit of control over the food. Beverley was a big fan of a meat chop with boiled veg and gravy. Diana had grown up eating a greater variety of dishes, but it seemed Beverley had developed narrower tastes as she'd got older. She'd hoped for something different at the alumni dinner last night, but it was always going to be a meat and gravy meal. It was that sort of place.

"Is there something different you'd like to eat?" asked Bev.

"Oh, no. Not especially," Diana lied.

"I could do us a spag bol or make a pie or something if you like?"

Diana wanted to suggest lightening the carb load, but didn't know where to start. "You know what, maybe I could get us something fancy from one of the food halls? Sometimes I get a really nice salad and a piece of spicy chicken."

"Nothing spicy for me, love. Can't handle it. Do they have plain roast chicken? I could maybe just have that. I'm not mad about salad either, unless it's a bit of tomato on a sandwich."

"Just chicken," said Diana. "There must be something that's a bit different you fancy?"

"No, not really. You have the thing you just said and I'll get a chop or something. I'll get one for you as well in case you don't have time to go and get your chicken."

"I can make time. Why would you get me a chop if I'm not eating it?"

Beverley shrugged. "It'll be fine tomorrow, won't it?"

"I don't want a chop tomorrow! I feel bloated with all the red meat and potato you pile on my plate."

Diana bit her tongue, but it was too late. Why did she always say the wrong thing?

Beverley put her spoon down and looked away. She carried the bowl out to the kitchen without another word.

"Mum! I'm sorry. I don't mean I don't like your cooking, I just want a bit less. I want a bit of variety."

"I get it love. You've grown away from your roots a bit, I reckon. You want one of them Mediterranean diets that they talk about on breakfast telly. Who can blame you, eh?"

Diana bristled. "It's not growing away from your roots if you want to eat healthily."

Her mum didn't reply. Diana watched her, guilt churning her stomach. How had food become such a battleground between them? They shouldn't be arguing like this. How were they supposed to share a living space if even the basics caused conflict?

CHAPTER FORTY-FIVE

When Zaf turned up for the morning run, Georg was waiting outside the changing room. He nodded a greeting.

"Morning Zaf! We're doing something a bit different today. I'll wait until your teammates are all here and then I'll explain."

"Right." Zaf wasn't sure what could be different about a morning run. He filled the time with a few warm up stretches. Jed and Parvani arrived a minute later. Then Josephine and her team arrived. They all stood in a loose group, waiting for Georg.

"This exercise will test your teamwork and your ability to flex your tour guide patter," Georg told them. "It's a deceptively simple task but one to which I will pay close attention. As two from each group undertake the morning run, the one who's left here with me will talk about a given topic for the exact amount of time that the run takes. You can have a few minutes to prepare what you want to say. I'm looking for a talk with a beginning, a middle and an end, and I want the timing to be as close as you can get it."

Zaf, Jed and Parvani looked at each other.

"Discuss it in your groups," Georg said. "You need to decide who will be doing the talk today. It will be about King Charles."

Parvani beckoned Jed and Zaf into a quiet corner. "I think we can ace this. I've kept a spreadsheet of our timings for the morning run and we average at twelve minutes and twenty seconds, so —"

"A spreadsheet?" Zaf waved his hand. He didn't know why he was surprised. "Yep. Fine. Go on."

"So if we are allowed a timer to monitor ourselves speaking, then we set it to count down twelve minutes twenty and then we do a visual check. If we're speaking here, then I think we probably have around eight seconds from when we can see the others coming to when they get here."

"Twelve minutes twenty," said Jed. "Got it. Who's going first with the talk?"

Parvani hesitated.

"What is it, Parvani?"

"I was going to say that I would do it, but you two could undoubtedly run round faster without me, so it might affect the timing."

"We'll keep the same pace. We'll run as if you're with us," said Jed.

Zaf and Jed set off together. They trotted along, talking to each other and concentrating hard on the muscle memory that suggested the right pace, even if they had a bit more speed to spare. As they left they heard Parvani starting to talk about King Charles and his interest in environmental issues.

"I can feel a weird panic that makes me want to go faster to put Parvani out of her misery," said Jed about halfway round.

"Me too, but we must resist. We're doing fine."

As they turned the final corner, they caught Parvani's eye. She ran to join them, her talk finished.

"Well done team," Georg said. "That was..." He glanced at Parvani. "You're right on time. Full marks."

They all took a seat while Josephine's team had their turn.

Parvani whispered to Zaf. "You know how Josephine shouts and bullies them to go round at top speed? What's going to happen now?"

Josephine was doing the talk, which was about the BBC. Sacha and Adi were doing the run.

Zaf could see her timer set for nine minutes and thirty seconds. The talk was little more than Josephine listing all the TV shows she could bring to mind. Zaf's own mind started to drift. It was dull.

Then Josephine's phone sounded a loud alarm.

"Oh, that was supposed to be on silent." Josephine looked over where she expected her teammates to emerge, but there was no sign of them.

She started to list other broadcasting companies and their contributions. It was excruciating.

When Sacha and Adi finally rounded the corner, Zaf breathed a sigh of relief.

"Well done, team," Georg said. "Although the timing of your two activities was out by quite a way, and your talk could have had more...substance Josephine. We'll be repeating this exercise, so you can refine your skills."

Josephine's team were awarded less than half the available marks. She walked away towards the rear of the Guild building. Georg didn't acknowledge her departure. Everyone glanced at each other nervously. Sacha and Adi exchanged worried whispers.

There was a fearsome grunting and then an enormous crashing sound.

Georg sighed. "I think I'd better see what that was."

He walked in the direction Josephine had gone. After a moment, everyone else followed.

They found Josephine emerging from a service yard at the back, pushing past them.

Georg was staring at a dumpster bin, folded almost in half. An enormous kerbstone was slammed down on top of it, embedded deep in the crumpled top.

Zaf looked at the kerbstone. How had Josephine even lifted it? "You reckon you could lift that?" he asked Jed.

Jed shook his head. "We could maybe just about lift it between us, but we wouldn't be able to throw it."

"Back to work, everyone. I'll need to do something about this, but it shouldn't distract us from our learning," said Georg.

Zaf looked at Sacha and Adi. They looked more than distracted. He could hear them discussing what Josephine might have to say about the speed of their run. What was that look? Fear.

He was on edge for the rest of the day's training.

"Should we all go out for a drink and celebrate our success?" Jed asked. "I feel like it was a bit eclipsed by Josephine's tantrum, but we did good."

"I have some reading to do," Parvani said. "I don't have the benefit of your youth, remember! You two go. You're right Jed, we did good today."

Zaf and Jed went to the Rising Sun, a nearby pub. They stood outside, watching the world go by with their drinks in their hands.

"Josephine was a bit of a beast today," Jed said.

"Putting it mildly." Zaf shook his head. "She bullies Sacha and Adi. I hope Georg keeps an eye on them."

"Yeah. You're right. You're like Mr Empathy or something."

"Empathy Man!" Zaf laughed. "It's a rubbish superpower, really."

"I don't know. Someone who puts others' feelings first is a superhero in my book. You should get an outfit, something form-fitting."

Jed traced an imaginary logo on Zaf's chest, making Zaf's skin tingle. Jed's eyes flicked down towards Zaf's lips and he leaned in to kiss him.

Jed was cute, that was beyond doubt.

What if Zaf let the moment take him? Why shouldn't he enjoy Jed's company in a more intimate way?

No.

He pulled away. "Jed, you're amazing. But can we... can we stay as just friends? Alexsei and me, it's a long-term thing, I'm certain of it."

Jed raised an eyebrow. "You sure about that? It seems like you two have problems."

"And that's just it. Even though I'm still mad at him about the flat, I know he's the person I want to be with."

"What does the billionaire's son have that I don't have, eh?"

Zaf frowned. "No —"

"Kidding. Hey, listen it was worth a flutter, you're quite the cutie. We'll never speak of this again, unless it's amusing or appropriate. Drink up, I'm going to get another."

CHAPTER FORTY-SIX

ZAF, Jed and Parvani sat in a nervous huddle. Today was the day they would find out their final project. Josephine's group also looked on edge, but Zaf wasn't sure if that was due to fear of the project or fear of Josephine.

Carolyn, Dr Blackthorn and Georg stood at the front of the lecture room. Carolyn swept an arm across the room. "Let's talk about your final project. Some of you might already know that we're looking for something original. Tourism in London is always changing. Where will you take it next? You have the best possible grounding, but can you impress us at the Guild?"

Zaf looked at Parvani and Jed. Could they?

Dr Blackthorn said, "We want you to come up with a half day tour that showcases any aspect of London you like. It has to be in some way novel. Use the rest of this session to exchange some initial ideas."

The groups moved to the sides of the room, as far apart as they could get.

"It's hard to think up new things," Parvani said. "Where do we start?"

"It's about getting people to pay attention and keeping them engaged," said Zaf. "Think about things that grabbed our attention recently, and how they kept our interest."

Jed gave him a look. Zaf pushed aside the distraction.

"Good idea," Parvani said. "There are those digital billboards that catch your eye by moving or talking to you when you pass."

"They're a bit creepy," Jed said.

"I dunno, did I see one that points out planes flying overhead?" Zaf said.

"Sounds expensive." Parvani signalled to Carolyn. "Is there any kind of budget available for this?"

Carolyn shook her head. "Only what you think you can charge for the tickets. If you take a group of five and cost the tickets at twenty pounds each, then your budget is a hundred pounds and the Guild will pay that. But we're not made of money."

When Carolyn had moved away, they leant in again. "Nothing as fancy as that will work," Parvani said. "Who else has thoughts on this?"

Jed sat up. "I saw some chalk captions on the pavement recently. Someone had identified the weeds growing there by putting the names next to them. It was really sweet."

"Ohh, an urban plant safari." Parvani nodded. "It would be great as long as it didn't rain. How about you, Zaf?"

Zaf thought. "It's not obviously about tourism, but the things that have grabbed my attention recently have been smells. They can transport you to a certain time and place like nothing else."

He realised he had Marek's candle from the room in his pocket right now.

Jed pointed at him. "You're not wrong. Whenever I smell lavender, it reminds me of my nan."

Parvani nodded. "Second-hand bookshops have that amazing smell. It feels like a nostalgia tour would work well with scent."

Zaf thought. "It's a shortcut to evoke a past era. The guy who lived in the flat above Diana's where I was staying had these amazing vintage fashions. Sometimes I would catch the slightest hint of old perfume from them."

"Are you thinking of a tour based around London's vintage fashion scene, with accompanying smells?" Jed said. "That would be fun."

Parvani grinned. "We need a nose."

Zaf and Jed looked at each other. They all had noses.

"A *nose*! A parfumier. Someone who really knows about smells."

"Sounds like it might be expensive," Jed said. "Hello, I am a Kardashian and I would like my own perfume line please and thank you."

Zaf nodded. "Maybe. But I'm guessing a parfumier is a person. Maybe we can find one through our extended network. If we can find one who's a friend of a friend, then they might give us some free advice. Everyone think hard about who we might know."

While the planning session continued, the three lecturers circled the room. When Georg came near, Zaf excused himself from the group to speak to him.

"Georg, can I pick your brains about something?"

Georg adjusted his spectacles and peered over them at Zaf. "Yes?"

Zaf felt warmer. "I read your book."

"My book?"

"The one about the Ludgate Candlesticks."

Georg looked blank, then nodded. "It was a very long time ago." He cocked his head. "These questions – they have nothing to do with your tour plans, do they?"

Zaf looked at him. "I just happen to think something might have happened to the candlesticks."

"Happened?"

"Zaf! We need your help on this," Jed called to him.

Zaf turned to Georg. "Sorry, I've got to..." He rejoined his group.

"We're stumped on finding a parfumier," Jed said. "If we just phone one up, a consultation is going to cost hundreds, if not thousands."

"We need to ask around," Parvani said.

"Does your super-rich boyfriend know any?" Jed asked Zaf.

Zaf brought up Alexsei's number and sent him a message to ask if he was free to talk. A moment later, his phone rang.

"Hi," said Zaf.

"Hi there." Alexsei's breathing was audible, like he was walking.

"I wonder if you minded me asking you something."

"Anytime. Shoot."

Zaf felt a pang of warmth. "I am on my way to meet my father, but I've got some time."

Zaf felt the coolness again. He was committed to rebuilding things with Alexsei, but the thought of Kamran Dadashov and what he had done to Diana still hurt.

"I wondered if you happened to know a parfumier."

Zaf hadn't expected the warm laughter.

"You live the strangest life."

"Do I?"

"Mmmm. You want her details?"

Zaf breathed out. "Thank you."

CHAPTER FORTY-SEVEN

DIANA HAD RUN three tours that week.

The Thursday morning tour had been a royal walking tour, including the changing of the guard and Buckingham Palace. Tourists had the capacity to surprise her with their questions, but the same favourite subjects always returned. 'What's under those big hats they wear?' 'Where do the horses sleep at night?' 'Are they real soldiers or just pretend?'

She never tired of the questions. Never tired of helping people understand her city.

She walked into the bus depot at Chartwell and Crouch before noon. Two buses sat inside; the third had already gone off to its new owners. It was odd how a massive warehouse depot could seem so empty for the lack of one bus.

Newton was in the kitchen area, reading the newspaper over a bowl of soup. Gus lay on the floor, perfectly still.

"Is he all right?" Diana said.

"He's dead," Newton replied.

"He's what?"

"At least I think that's the plan." Newton peered round to

inspect the lifeless cat. "Yes, I think he's pretending to be dead as some sort of protest."

"The diet is still continuing?"

"It's not a diet as such. He's reaped the rewards of living a double life and now he must pay a little back. Can't have our boy being just another fat and pampered cat."

Diana thought that's exactly what Gus was. But she kept quiet.

"You will note this is vegetable soup." Newton pointed with his spoon. "To help him stay on the straight and narrow, I'm not bringing in any meat or fish foods for the time being. Just in case you were planning on doing so."

"I'm off out for lunch today, actually."

"Nice for some."

"An old friend. We're meeting at Refugio's up by Baker Street station."

"Posh."

"It's a friend with certain standards."

"Soup and abstinence are good enough for Gus and me."

Refugio's was a Portuguese restaurant that had been serving locals and visitors for over two decades. When she'd suggested meeting up somewhere near her work, it was one of the first places Pascal had mentioned.

He was waiting on the pavement outside the restaurant. His handsome face cracked into a smile as he saw her approach. It was funny how people aged, somehow both changing utterly and yet remaining the same. Like a city, surface elements changed but the character of the landscape stayed somehow in place.

He wore a pale linen suit, his trademark for the last twenty years. The lines in his face had deepened. And yet, in that smile, there was still the charming and fiercely clever rogue she had met when she was little more than a teenager.

He bowed slightly to plant a kiss on her cheek.

The waiting staff showed them to a table by the window. The restaurant name and the words 'Doces Portugueses Autênticos' were stencilled on the window, reversed now they were inside.

The waiter left menus and when asked what they would like to drink, and both of them said, "Just water" at the same time. Pascal had fought with alcoholism for many years and, to the best of Diana's knowledge, had been sober for two decades.

"How long has it been since we've done this?" he said.

"A long time."

"Your last birthday party was an all too fleeting opportunity to catch up."

"Made all the more awkward by Ariadne turning up."

He shrugged at the mention of his ex. "Even hatred is worn down into something familiar and comforting as the years go by. Would you believe me if I said I missed her?"

Diana shook her head. "Sometimes we're better off alone."

The waiter approached, notepad at the ready. Diana generally hated it when people ordered for the table without asking. But when dining out with a semi-retired restaurant critic, it was always a good idea to let him take charge.

He ordered caldo verde to start, with mains of bacalhau à brás and a bifana sandwich for himself.

As the green soup, dotted with chorizo, was set before them, Pascal said, "So, you've been visiting Morris?"

There was a critical tone in his voice. Their days in the music business and the whirlwind of fun, hard work, money and heartache that had been ElectraBeat had inextricably tangled their lives together. Pascal knew Morris perhaps as well as any man on earth, and he had not forgiven his old bandmate for his crimes against the company Diana worked for.

"I do visit Morris. There is no one else."

Pascal took a delicate spoonful of the soup. "How is he?"

Diana broke a piece of the complimentary bread. "If I said 'good' I would be lying. But he's found... a rhythm, a pace, a place. He's doing as well as a man nearing his seventies can do in prison."

Pascal nodded. "It must be hard on you."

"Hard on me how?"

He waggled his eyebrows. "Prison. Tough and scary places."

She tilted her head. "I think I can be a tough and scary woman if I want to."

He laughed. "You and my ex! What cloth did they cut you two from, eh?"

"The East End breeds tough women."

"And how is your mother?"

And with that she let it all out, the story of how she had come to live with her mum in a small Bromley-by-Bow flat. And if she was going to mention living with her mum, she couldn't talk to Pascal about it without mentioning her mum's attitude to food.

"War-time generation," he said. "Grew up believing every meal could be their last and that the more fat, sugar and salt you had on the plate the better."

"The war was eighty years ago!"

"People never change."

Diana's main was a flavoursome codfish dish mixed with onions, potatoes and eggs. Pascal's was a massive sandwich, surely too big for one person, which he dissected with his knife and fork.

"Red plates," he said out of nowhere.

"Sorry?" she said.

He tapped the edge of her colourful plate with his knife. "Buy your mum red plates. Or any dark single colour plate. I bet her plates are white."

"They are."

"We see a white space and there's something about the human psyche that wants to fill it. We pile on the food. If there's colour already there, we're not so tempted to pile it on."

"Is that true?"

"Buy your mum some red plates and the massive portions of carbs will go down. Trust me."

Diana thought on this.

"You want my opinion on Morris's supposed alibi, don't you?" Pascal said. "He's adding more details. What was it? A fluffy Pomeranian?"

"Called Marengo."

Pascal waved his fork around. "Details. Filling the plate. He's stringing you along, Diana. Piling more and more on because underneath it all, the plate is white, the story an empty nonsense."

"Cute."

"Me?"

"You always had a way with words."

"They are my bread and meat, in more than one sense."

"You don't believe him at all, then?"

Pascal put down his cutlery and grasped her hands across the table. He had an old man's hands, now. Maybe she had an old woman's hands.

"Morris was my friend, my very, very best friend," he said. "I loved him. I do love him. I have nothing but love for him. But

I know him. He was greedy. He was always greedy. Which of us profited most from the music royalties?"

She nodded. After all the other ElectraBeat members had cashed in on their success, Morris Walker had reinvested and come out with enough to make him comfortable for life.

"He could smell out money," she agreed.

"He was tight with it, too. Right now, he'd be questioning why you and I are paying top dollar for what is essentially a fish pie and a hot pork sandwich."

She laughed and extracted her hand from his to reach for her water glass.

"A café around a corner from a hotel," he said. "In a city with a thousand hotels and even more cafés. It's an unfalsifiable lie. A desperate gambit." He speared a piece of pork on his fork.

She eyed him. "Please, let's talk of happier things instead."

CHAPTER FORTY-EIGHT

ALEXSEI DID INDEED KNOW a parfumier and, on Friday, was happy to make introductions. Zaf walked with Jed and Parvani from St Paul's to Covent Garden to meet him at the parfumier's, passing the Law Courts and Chancery on their way.

"We should think about our audience," said Parvani as they walked. "Who would come on this tour?"

"Fashion students and fashion fans?" suggested Zaf. "People who were there and want to remember what it was like?"

"If we're going back to the sixties," said Jed, "then the people who were part of the fashion scene are getting quite old now."

Parvani nodded. "So we should focus more on education than nostalgia. We look at the sixties, talking about the youth movement. We've got Mary Quant's shop in Chelsea and the Biba shop in Kensington." She scrolled through her phone. "It looks as though there was a nightclub called Sibylla's near Piccadilly Circus that was a big part of the swinging sixties scene. The Beatles and the Stones turned up for the launch, and loads of other famous names."

Jed nodded. "What do we have for the early seventies?"

"We could do worse than talk about Bowie," said Zaf.

"Perfect!" said Parvani. "Then we're onto punk, and Vivienne Westwood's shop, back in Chelsea. Maybe we can make it a circular tour?" She traced an outline in the air, picturing it on a map.

"Is fashion in the sixties and seventies the scope of our tour?" asked Zaf. "There's already a lot to talk about."

Jed nodded. "Yeah."

"Reckon so," said Parvani. "Now we need to figure out what scents will evoke each of these times and places."

"We should talk to some people who were around at the time," said Zaf. "See what they can remember."

"Good idea," said Parvani. "Let's see what we can come up with by tomorrow, shall we?"

Alexsei's parfumier friend, Angeline, had a counter located inside a larger shop that sold expensive face creams and bath products. Alexsei was already waiting for them. He kissed Zaf's cheek as the three trainee tour guides approached the counter, and Zaf gave him a smile.

The counter and the area behind it was made of tinted glass shelving backed with mirrors and discreet lighting. Exquisite bottles were arrayed alongside subtle packaging. While Angeline served a customer, Zaf tried to imagine what each scent was like. A striped box with bright colours made him think of fresh Mediterranean citrus, while another with a dark, earthy design must surely be rich and spicy. He shuffled over to look at a box that reminded him of Moroccan tiles and exotic flowers while Jed seemed drawn to one that looked like leather trimmed with hedge cuttings.

"Welcome to Angeline's sensory adventures!" Angeline was dressed in a lab coat made of powder-blue linen and had her hair pinned up neatly. "I think we can step upstairs for a few minutes."

She led the way to a workshop space modelled like a science lab, with bottles of perfume ingredients arrayed in rows.

It took all of Zaf's self-control not to start lifting glass stoppers from the tops of the bottles so that he could sniff things like civet, vanilla and jasmine.

"Take a seat and tell me what your plans are," said Angeline.

"We're students at the Guild of Tourism and we have an idea for our final project that we'd love some advice on," said Parvani. "Actually, it was Zaf who came up with it."

Zaf nodded. "We want to use scent to make our visitors feel transported to a particular place and time. We wondered about a link to fashion, maybe? A tour that takes in important London fashion hotspots, perhaps?"

Angeline looked excited at the idea. "When you say scent, do you specifically mean a commercial fragrance, or were you thinking of a broader olfactory experience?"

"What do you mean?" Zaf asked.

"Well most of the fashion designers will have launched one or more fragrances. It's even possible to track things like feminism through commercial fragrances, but it's a story that spans many decades. If you were thinking more specifically of taking people back to the days of the Swinging Sixties, then you might start off with the scent of stale beer. I'm willing to bet that most of England smelled of stale beer and smoke from domestic fires back then." She shrugged. "I'm guessing, of course, I wasn't there myself. Then as you move forward, we'd get some cannabis and patchouli mixed in as young people started to exercise a little more freedom and rebellion. That type of thing, yeah?"

"Yeah!" Zaf's mind reeled with the possibilities. He looked at Jed and Parvani. "What d'you think?"

"How would we even make the smell of stale beer?" asked Jed.

"I can make the smell of most things you can think of," said Angeline. "Pop it in an atomiser and you can spray a little cloud for your guests to walk through or sniff. Your best bet would be to work out your icons and locations, then we can workshop what the olfactory experience might be, and we're on our way."

Zaf looked at the array of bottles on the workbench and pictured himself trying to create the smell of punk or house music. "It sounds brilliant. Are you sure you don't mind helping us? We don't really have a budget for this."

Angeline shrugged. "I can play the long game. Sooner or later you'll have a group that wants a perfume workshop, and you'll bring them here."

"We will," said Zaf. "Can I smell some of these?"

"Yes. Do prepare yourself, though."

Zaf's hand hovered over the bottle labelled *civet*. "Why?"

"That one there's pretty disgusting in the concentrated form. When it's diluted right down it smells amazing."

Zaf gave a tentative sniff. "Ugh!" He put the top back on and placed the bottle down. "It's like...ugh. It's like drains." He took in gasps of air.

Angeline laughed. "Welcome to my world. Scent is never dull."

Remembering, Zaf dipped into his inside jacket pocket and pulled out the candle. "I found this in my room the other day."

Angeline inspected the candle that had fallen down the back of the chest of drawers. She sniffed. "Frankincense."

"Is it?"

She nodded. "Or olibanum if you like."

"Frankincense as in, gold, frankincense and myrrh?"

"That's the stuff. Quite a religious smell, isn't it? The best stuff comes from Arabia but..." She sniffed again. "This is Coptic frankincense. From a different tree. *Boswellia frereana.* A less heavy scent. Most of it comes from Somalia and is sold in Egypt."

Zaf looked at her. "Egypt?"

Georg had returned from Egypt only weeks before, the day before Marek's death.

Was that a coincidence, or something more?

CHAPTER FORTY-NINE

Diana opened the door to Zaf that evening. "Come in!"

"Who's that?" Beverley shouted.

"It's Zaf," Diana replied. "I'll put the kettle on."

"Come on in and help me with the sky parts, Zaf!" Beverley said. "With a pair of fresh eyes on it, we'll soon have this jigsaw done."

Diana brought in the drinks to find Zaf bent over the jigsaw.

"I came to ask you both for some help with a project I'm working on," Zaf said. "It's probably mostly a question for Bev, though. It's about the smells of London in the sixties and seventies."

"Do you mean the perfumes you could get?" Beverley asked.

"No, more like the everyday smells."

"Oh right." Beverley thought for a moment. "I swear everything smelt stronger in those days. The river could be pretty stinky, especially in summer. There was a lot of pollution. The soap had a strong smell too."

"Carbolic?" Diana said with a smile. "You can still get it, you know?"

"We should get some, it was good stuff. You knew you were clean because you smelt clean. Everyone's uncle smelt of Brylcreem, of course."

"What did that smell like?" Zaf asked.

"Brylcreem? I dunno, something like posh soap crossed with furniture polish."

Zaf stabbed some notes into his phone. "Great stuff!"

"I was a young child in the sixties," Diana said, "and women didn't use as many products as people would these days. But I did always have a sniff of Ponds cold cream or Nivea if I went exploring someone's dressing table. Ponds was a bit bland, like baby powder with the tiniest hint of rose. Nivea wasn't that different, but a bit more floral."

"We used to let you have a dab of cream on your nose." Beverley laughed.

"I remember the smell of Germolene antiseptic on a cut, and disinfectant when someone had been cleaning."

"Wax polish was a lot more popular then," Beverley said. "Shops used to smell of it because there was more wood. Brasso too, on the handles and suchlike."

Diana nodded. "What are you thinking for the tour then, Zaf?"

"We're looking at the fashion hotspots from the sixties and seventies. Maybe a circular tour with little atomisers to add smells."

"That sounds fascinating," said Diana. "Well, you'll definitely want patchouli and sandalwood once you get to the later sixties and early seventies. They were the signature smells of hippies."

"I thought that was body odour and cannabis." Beverley

narrowed her eyes. "There was that young tyke down the road called Lenny who dressed in that filthy coat. I swear he didn't wash after about sixty-eight. It's all very well having peace and love, but a bit of Lifebuoy wouldn't have gone amiss."

"Lifebuoy?" Zaf asked.

"Another soap. Pop it on your list, it was like the carbolic soap, but it got updated to smell a bit more like a pine forest, as I recall."

As Diana and her mum dredged up their memories of smells from homes, shops and public places, Zaf alternated between notetaking and placing jigsaw pieces.

"Would you look at that," Beverley said. "He's only gone and finished the sky while we were talking."

Zaf grinned. "You have been massively helpful. Mmmm, speaking of smells." He produced the candle that all but lived in his pocket now. "The candle from Marek's room."

Beverley took it and sniffed it. "Frankincense."

"Not only that," Zaf said with the enthusiasm of a person who'd just learned something. "It's a kind of frankincense mostly sold in Egypt."

"Where Georg has recently returned from?" Diana said.

"Who's Georg?" her mum asked.

"A lecturer at the Guild of Tourism," Zaf said.

Diana frowned. "So both Georg's book and a candle that came from the country Georg had just returned from were found in Marek's room? Did Marek steal them both?"

Beverley put a piece of jigsaw into place. "Are you two still sticking your noses into deaths that have nothing to do with you? I thought you and that Pascal Palmer were working on clearing Morris's name."

Zaf gave Diana a questioning look, and for a fleeting instant she felt a touch of girlish embarrassment.

"Pascal and I met for lunch today. Morris had provided me with another nugget relating to his alibi. A Pomeranian dog called Marengo, of all things. I wanted to pick Pascal's brains over what to do about it. Apart from making crockery suggestions, he was not overly helpful."

"You and Pascal get on well, don't you?" Zaf said.

"He's an old friend."

"Handsome, too."

Beverley laughed. "She could do far worse."

"He's nearly seventy, Mum."

"You're no spring chicken either."

"I remember," Diana said, raising her voice, "a certain someone who was horrified that as teenagers Ariadne and I were hanging around with two men in their twenties."

"Age gaps mean less when you get to your age."

"My age," Diana tutted.

"What's this thing about crockery?" Zaf said.

Diana patted her mum's hand. "I'm buying Mum some new plates, for the sake of my sanity and waistline."

"I'm sure I don't understand."

"Ah!" Beverley put another piece in the puzzle.

CHAPTER FIFTY

Paul Kensington strode into the little kitchen at Chartwell and Crouch, his face scrunched up like he'd sniffed sour milk.

It wasn't often you saw the depot manager in here. His office was his kingdom, complete with a big desk, a posh coffee machine and a tiny Japanese sand garden. The kitchen was different: chipped mugs, a huge teapot and more biscuits than you could shake a stick at. The two worlds didn't mix.

"What is wrong with that man?" Paul said.

Diana had been sipping her tea, working out her next move. Gus sat on her knee, hoping for a scrap of biscuit. No chance, not with him being on a diet.

She'd just got an email from Carolyn Desanti. Zaf's graduation ceremony was next week. She'd replied to say she'd be there. The mystery of the dead homeless bloke and the dodgy candles might have to take a back seat.

"What man?" she replied. Then it clicked. "Newton? Are you asking me why he's sad? I should think it's because...

because we sold off one of his buses this week. And we're selling another one tomorrow. He's heartbroken."

Paul frowned. "They're not his buses. I've not sold *his* buses."

"They are his. He's looked after them for years. He's kept them running, kept them..." She shrugged. "They're like family to him."

Paul shook his head. "They're company buses."

"And he's been their carer. Like a foster parent. They've gone to new owners, but he doesn't see it like that."

"They're not people. They're not even..." He waved a hand at Gus. "They're not even animals."

"They're more important than that to him. Have you never spoken to him? Newton has a human family. How he found room in his heart for bus..." She shook her head. "But it's his little fleet that means the most to him. And we're taking that away."

Paul glared. "I'm not having him moping about the place. Moping is not the Chartwell and Crouch way."

He marched out. Gus lifted his head, wondering what the racket was about.

"There, there." Diana stroked him.

She pulled out her phone and made a call.

"DCI Clint Sugarbrook."

"Detective Chief Inspector," she said. "I hope I'm not interrupting something."

"Always, Miss Bakewell. How can I help you?"

"I have information. It might seem... tangential."

"Every time you come near one of my cases, it creates more work for me."

"It's about the candlesticks in St Paul's Cathedral."

"That's completely unrelated."

"Not at all. In his room, Marek Bogacki left behind a book about them. Zaf and I both suspect the candlesticks in the Cathedral are fakes."

There was a sigh. "That's your big insight."

"Zaf has looked at the book, written by Georg Strandman, the Guild lecturer. The pictures in there and the real candlesticks aren't the same."

"So Marek is now a master forger."

"My role is not to present a theory but to tell you what I know."

"You stick your nose in and make things twice as complicated." A half-laugh. "Fine. Leave it with me. We might take a look."

"Thank you, Detective Chief Inspector."

She ended the call and rubbed between Gus's ears. The cat let out a happy 'meep'.

"We do what we can, don't we?" she said.

CHAPTER FIFTY-ONE

When Zaf went to the Guild the next day, he was full of ideas for their tour. But he and Jed found Parvani in a state of extreme anxiety.

"I heard Josephine talking on the phone," she told them. "Her brother owns a tech firm. He's building her an app that uses augmented reality for her tour."

Zaf and Jed stared at her.

"It means her group will beat ours," she said. "What are we going to do?"

"We're going to stick to our guns and make our tour the best it can be," Zaf said.

"It's a good idea," Jed added. "We can make this work."

"Let's compare notes," Parvani said.

"We should get it all into a spreadsheet," Jed said. "You'll feel better when it's all captured in a spreadsheet."

"Definitely. Let's do it."

They spent a couple of hours in the Guild library, then prepared to head out to meet the parfumier. As he left the library, Zaf heard voices in the museum next door.

"It would be sad to lose you, Georg."

Zaf stepped into the museum. It was full of eclectic collections in glass cases. Many of the exhibits were linked to the Guild's history as the headquarters of the parish constables.

Without making himself visible, Zaf watched Georg Strandman and Carolyn Desanti talking as they stood in front of a cabinet of fine silverware.

"...this place would always be your home," Carolyn was saying.

"And it is, it is," Georg replied. "But perhaps I need a quieter pace of life, a chance to explore this country while I still have strength in my bones."

Carolyn nodded. "Look at this. Sixteenth century silverware. Do you remember this, Georg? I think you helped to catalogue it. Worth at least ten thousand pounds and we don't even protect it with a decent security system. Maybe we should sell it off to fund the Guild for another six months, but it's too precious to us."

Georg said nothing. Carolyn placed a hand on his arm.

Jed tugged on Zaf's sleeve. "Come on! Thought we'd left you behind!"

Zaf followed him out into the sunshine and the team set off westward through London.

Forty-five minutes later, Zaf, Jed and Parvani sat with Angeline in her workshop.

"We have a lot to get through," Angeline said. "First of all, your spreadsheet was a tremendous help. I wish all of my clients were as organised and thoughtful as you."

She handed Zaf, Jed and Parvani six tiny bottles, each containing a scent. The labels read *Quant, Biba, Carnaby, Sibylla, Bowie* and *Punk*.

"These are working titles. Shall we go through them in order? Take the top off *Quant* and I'll walk you through it."

Zaf removed the top and bent over to sniff it.

"Careful," Angeline said. "They're very concentrated. Let it breathe for a moment."

"Phenols?" Jed said.

"From disinfectants," Parvani added.

"That's right. The phenols will be barely detectable at first sniff, but will linger as a raw, leathery tang. What do you detect in the high notes?"

"A sweet shop?" Zaf said.

Angeline nodded. "It speaks of the playful youth vibe."

They moved onto *Biba,* with its grand art deco scents.

"Let's examine *Carnaby* shall we?"

Zaf sniffed it. "Diesel."

"There's also a peppermint note..."

"...urban, so diesel is something I tried to capture."

"Newton, my colleague will love this. He's a big fan of vintage vehicles."

Sibylla contained sandalwood to evoke London's high society.

"*Bowie* then. The music scene of the early seventies..."

"...bacon?" Zaf said.

Angeline laughed. "A lot of informal meetings took place in cafes along there, so..."

"Bacon. You're like a magician of smell," Jed said.

"Onto the final one. We're back in Chelsea to talk about Vivienne Westwood and punk."

Zaf removed the top and sniffed it. "...metal."

"Superglue."

"Sweat."

Angeline laughed. "You lot are a perfect olfactory audience. There's a slight sweaty tang..."

"This is going to be so good," Parvani said. "We can create some sort of a Look Book to show examples of the fashions we're describing."

"I can put each scent into an atomiser," Angeline said. "What do you all think?"

"I think we're going to blow everyone away," Jed said.

Zaf nodded. "And I think I'll finally have a chance to wear the amazing vintage stripy suit I was given a while ago. It throws off some serious Bowie vibes."

Angeline handed Zaf, Jed and Parvani atomisers filled with the scents. "You can create a small cloud while you're doing the tour."

"I love them," Parvani said. "Thank you."

"I'm very happy that you like them."

CHAPTER FIFTY-TWO

Zaf, Parvani and Jed met in the classroom at the Guild building. Zaf wore the suit that he had christened the Bowie suit, which on the hanger simply looked like a multicoloured striped lycra two piece with a zipped top. Once it was on a human, though, the outlandish silhouette became obvious. The contrast collar and extended epaulettes had brought a smile to his face as he examined himself in the mirror.

"Check you out!" said Jed with a whoop of glee.

"You too." Jed had found a psychedelic shirt that he wore over skinny jeans.

"And here comes Parvani, looking every inch the badass punk that we all knew she was."

"Stop it." She wore an asymmetrical tartan dress with black tights and boots featuring buckles and studs. The three of them had scoured local charity shops until they found the elements of an outfit that Parvani felt comfortable in.

"We all look amazing," said Zaf.

"Josephine's group's coming," said Jed.

They all pretended not to look as Josephine, Sacha and Adi walked in wearing matching outfits. They wore fitted lilac jumpsuits, and looked ready either to pilot a space ship or present a kids' TV show, Zaf wasn't sure which.

Josephine led her group over so that she could face off with Parvani. "You do know that the three of you look like freaks, don't you? We're supposed to be tour guides. What on earth is this?" She flicked a finger nail at Zaf's zip, which was undone to just below his Adam's apple.

"Huh, she's right," said Jed. "It should be down here I reckon." He pulled the zip down six inches and made an appreciative click. "Better. We aim to please our clients, after all."

"Good grief." Josephine stalked away, with Sacha and Adi trailing behind her.

"Is it me, or do Sacha and Adi look slightly embarrassed to be cosplaying the Pink Ladies from Grease?" Jed asked.

"I think they might actually be embarrassed by Josephine," said Parvani. "I feel bad for them. They didn't ask to be selected by her."

"Put them from your mind until the tour is over," said Jed. "For now, we must focus."

Georg arrived and smiled around the classroom. "As you very well know, this is the day of the tour. To keep things impartial, I won't be your client. One group will have Doctor Blackthorn and the other will have Carolyn. They are waiting for each group to take them on the tour you have designed. Parvani, your group will take Carolyn, and Josephine, your group will take Doctor Blackthorn."

They went outside to collect their clients. As they came out into churchyard, Zaf saw Detective Chief Inspector Sugarbrook and his sergeant, Quigley, striding over from the entrance to Paternoster Square.

"Mr Strandman?" said the detective. "Could we borrow you for a moment?"

Georg looked alarmed.

"Just want to pick your brains a bit," said Sugarbrook. If that comment was meant to put Georg's mind at ease, it didn't appear to work.

Georg looked at Carolyn and Dr Blackthorn, alarmed. Carolyn gave him a helpless look. "We will follow our tour guides and see you later, Georg." She didn't add 'I hope' but Zaf strongly felt it was implied.

"Right, our taxi is this way," said Parvani brightly.

As they walked to the waiting cab, Zaf saw Diana waiting by the entrance to St Paul's Cathedral.

Sugarbrook and Diana?

Soon, Zaf, Jed and Parvani were in a taxi with Carolyn Desanti.

"We're using a taxi for the transport. If we were a larger group we'd obviously use a minibus or a coach," said Parvani. "It's a circular tour that will begin and end in Chelsea.

"Or we could use a vintage bus," added Zaf with a smile. He tried not to think about the lovely buses that Newton was preparing for sale.

On the way to Chelsea, they explained their tour's concept to Carolyn. She looked intrigued at the idea.

Zaf wondered how much she might remember of the sixties and seventies, and whether that would work in their favour. He thought that she was perhaps about Diana's age, so she would have some recollection of the sixties and probably better memories of the seventies.

The taxi driver dropped them at Markham Square, which was a residential square off the Kings Road. Zaf was reminded of the wonderful house at Eccleston Square that he and Diana had said goodbye to. He looked through the railings at the garden, and decided that it really wasn't as lovely as the garden at Eccleston Square.

"Here we are at our first location," said Parvani, leading Carolyn to a shop on the corner. "You will see a plaque on the wall up there. This shop was the location of Mary Quant's *Bazaar*, which is the first place we'd like to talk about on our olfactory tour of London's fashion hotspots. Jed, would you like to do the honours with the scent?"

Jed stepped slightly away from the group and puffed some of the scent out of the *Quant* atomiser. "Here we go. Would you like to take a little sniff?"

Zaf thought it was fortunate that it was a windless day, or they would have had to find somewhere sheltered to spray the scent. It hung obediently in the air so that they could all smell it, and they began to describe its various elements for Carolyn. Zaf held up the Look Book, so that everyone could easily picture the fashions as they talked through the first of their stories.

They all watched Carolyn carefully for a reaction, but she kept her face neutral until they had finished speaking.

"I must tell you," she said eventually, "that you're really onto something here. I would not have believed that you could actually transport me back to when I was very young, but you did it with that. I was too young to come to the shop, but the smell really spoke to me. Well done!"

Zaf grinned at Jed and Parvani. They were off to an excellent start.

"Let's move on to our next stop, then. We're off to visit the location of *Biba*."

Carolyn's eyes lit up. "Oh, I can't wait! The Biba look was just amazing."

Zaf thought that it was perhaps convenient they had ended up with her rather than Dr Blackthorn. He couldn't imagine the fusty professor having quite the same enthusiasm for vintage fashions.

CHAPTER FIFTY-THREE

Diana walked with Sugarbrook, Quigley and Georg into St Paul's Cathedral. Georg seemed alarmed to have been cornered by the police.

"Mr Strandman, I hope you don't mind us taking up your time," said the detective chief inspector. "We're hoping to lean upon your expertise a little."

"My expertise?" asked Georg.

"According to Miss Bakewell here, you are perhaps the world's foremost expert on the... what are they called?"

"The Ludgate Candlesticks," said Diana.

"Yes, those," said Sugarbrook. "And based upon your book, she has a theory that— ah!"

He stopped as a tall man with silver hair at his temples approached them. The man halted abruptly, making Diana think of the military, and put out a hand to shake with Sugarbrook and then Quigley.

"Amir Kambarzahi," he said. "Fortress Security Solutions."

Sugarbrook made swift introductions. "Thank you for

meeting with us. I hope we can get a clear answer to a few questions."

Mr Kambarzahi smiled at him. "If the question is 'have the Ludgate Candlesticks been stolen and replaced with forgeries?', you will find the answer a very simple no. This way, please."

They crossed the floor of the Cathedral. The sound of feet on the flagstones and the echoes that the dome threw back from the hundred or more people in the Cathedral always seemed to add to the holy air of the place. Off towards the altar, the sound of a church organ started up. Diana's own relationship with faith and religious belief was tenuous at best, but that didn't mean she couldn't be moved by the power of a religious space.

"In here." Mr Kambarzahi directed them into the exhibition space. The organ music was quieter here, but not by much.

Kambarzahi approached the candlesticks in their security case.

"You know about the Ludgate Candlesticks, then?" he asked Georg.

"I composed a short work about them many years ago," Georg replied. "Little more than a pamphlet, really." He stepped nearer and removed his spectacles to inspect the candlesticks and the display card on the wall beside them. "Have any of you read up on them?"

"Twelfth century," said Diana.

"Very good. Anything else?"

"They depict the story of the Rich Man and Lazarus from the Book of Luke."

"That's who these blokes are, then?" asked Quigley.

Diana gestured at the two men represented on the candlesticks. "A wealthy man and, living just outside his door, a poor man called Lazarus. The rich man had everything and the poor man had nothing, but then they died. Lazarus, poor in life, went on to receive his rewards in Heaven."

"Yes, thank you for the history lesson," said Sugarbrook. "I think we're all keen to know whether these are real."

"They're composed from a mixture of metals," said Georg, "including a significant hoard of what is commonly believed to be Saxon gold. Analysis was performed on them over twenty years ago."

"I read up on that," said Kambarzahi. "The team from the Guild of Tourism helped with it. They've been on display, mostly here, ever since."

"The questions we need to ask," said Sugarbrook, "is, are these the same candlesticks, and could they possibly have been replaced with fakes."

"I take pride in our company's work," Kambarzahi replied. "I don't like the suggestion we might have lost a valuable item under our care. So let me show you."

He took out a set of keys and inserted a stubby ring-headed key into the lock of the display case. As he slid the door aside there was a beeping from a panel on the wall and a light began to flash.

He pressed a button on his phone and spoke. "Carl. Beginning test."

He reached in and rocked one of the candlesticks on its base. The beep became a whooping alarm and a light on the wall began to flash. Kambarzahi steadied the candlestick.

"End test, Carl," he said into his phone. The siren wail became a beep once more. He closed and locked the cabinet and the room fell silent, all warning lights extinguished.

"If this hadn't been a test," said Kambarzahi, "then the police would be notified and here within minutes. A smash and grab artist might make it some distance from here, but who's going to run across London carrying five-pound candlesticks?"

"An effective demonstration," said Sugarbrook.

"Furthermore..." The security expert pointed towards the top corner of the room. Diana could see the glassy lens of a CCTV camera.

"Twenty-four-seven surveillance?" asked DS Quigley.

Kambarzahi nodded. "And with the help of our wonderful new AI footage analyst, I can tell you within seconds who has been near this case at any point in the last eight months. I can tell you if anyone has even put their hand inside it."

"Very impressive," said Diana.

"Who do you think stole the candlesticks? When?" asked Kambarzahi.

Sugarbrook looked pointedly at Diana. "A burglar called Marek Bogacki. He moved into a hostel in the area a couple of weeks ago. He died there."

"A security systems expert, was he? A hacker? Perhaps the kind of person to take a 3D rendering of the candlesticks, 3D print copies from which to make moulds, and then cast passable forgeries? That sort of person?"

"Nothing of the sort," said Sugarbrook.

"No," said Kambarzahi. "And on top of that, despite the almost incalculable value of these candlesticks, selling them on would be very difficult. The thief would need connections in the antiquities business, the dodgiest sort of connections."

"Apart from the last bit, this really doesn't sound like our Bogacki guy," said Quigley.

Sugarbrook turned to Georg. "Question is, are these fakes?"

Georg waved a hand airily. "To check properly, we would

need a chemical analysis of the material. But from the outside..." He stroked his chin. "These look like the real deal."

"OK," said Sugarbrook. "Then I think we shall call that conclusive."

He thanked Kambarzahi and Georg and led the way upstairs. The organist was in full flow now, layering powerful chord upon powerful chord. Georg excused himself and went off back to the Guild.

Diana watched him go.

"Detective Chief Inspector," she said, "why do I get the impression that you have arranged all of this purely to teach me a lesson?"

Sugarbrook rearranged the lapels of his thin trench coat. "Teach you a lesson, Miss Bakewell? Chance would be a fine thing. No, that needed to be done. If there was a lead to be had here, we would have followed it."

They stepped outside. It was a sunny day once again, bucking the stereotype of London as a constantly grey and drizzly city.

"There are over a hundred murders in London each year," Sugarbrook continued. "In nearly a third of them, we can't even identify a possible suspect. An even larger percentage never result in a successful conviction."

"You're saying that Marek Bogacki's murder is going to be unsolved."

Sugarbrook screwed up his face. He didn't like the idea any more than she did.

"People fall through the cracks in society," he said. "People get lost. People disappear. There are too many unsolved mysteries to bear thinking about. Chances are, we'll finish the paperwork on Marek Bogacki and he'll become one of those we can't help."

CHAPTER FIFTY-FOUR

ZAF, Jed and Parvani's taxi tour of London had reached its final stop. The cab pulled up on the Kings Road, further along from where they'd started. Carolyn stepped out onto the pavement with a smile.

"World's End, Vivienne Westwood's place!"

"That's right," said Parvani.

"I met her, you know," said Carolyn. "It was at a gallery opening. I think the artist was a friend of hers. Such a fascinating woman."

Zaf smiled. He'd become used to Diana surprising him with anecdotes like that, but to imagine Carolyn, who was most at home on the muddy foreshore of the Thames, meeting one of fashion's biggest names was mind-blowing.

"Your dress is an excellent homage to her style," Carolyn said to Parvani.

Parvani beamed.

They walked through the scent and flicked through the pages of the Look Book. It was clearly a big hit with Carolyn.

"You've even included the superglue. I was one of those

people who used it in my hair. It was thoroughly stupid of me. My mother went wild."

Parvani's gaze swivelled from Carolyn's face to the mohican hairstyles of the punks in the Look Book, as if she couldn't imagine the two images colliding.

"Marengo!"

Zaf's head turned. Carolyn was talking about something to do with fashion, but he wasn't listening.

"Marengo! Leave it alone!"

He scanned the pavement on the other side of the road. A woman in a brimmed hat tottered along and – Zaf couldn't see as a bus went by – there!

On a long lead behind her, moving at a very leisurely pace, was a big ball of white fluffiness.

"...and you will hear about the marks in the next day or two," Carolyn was saying.

"Excuse me a moment." Zaf gave an apologetic look to the others and made to cross the road. The traffic was non-stop and he had to find a gap between vehicles. He raced across, waving at a bus driver who braked to avoid running him down.

"Hey! Where are you going?" Jed called.

Zaf gestured down the road. "It's a dog! Marengo! It's a witness to a crime! Sort of!"

It was the best explanation he could give in the time available. What could he say? 'Diana's old boss is doing time for fraud because his alibi hinged upon an old lady in a café with a Pomeranian called Marengo'? That would just have led to further questions.

He ran down the pavement in the direction the old woman had gone. She couldn't have been far ahead, and yet there was no sign of her now.

He reached Sloane Square and looked around, the thick

traffic and crowds making it hard to see. Had she gone into one of the shops? Down an alley he'd not noticed? How had a slow old woman and her dog given him the slip so quickly?

Cursing, he did a circuit of the square before returning to find Jed and Parvani waiting for him on the pavement. The taxi had gone, taking Carolyn with it.

Jed and Parvani looked less than pleased.

"What the hell?" demanded Parvani.

"Sorry," said Zaf. "I... I had to go. If I told you a man's freedom depended on it, would you believe me?"

"What? No. That's mad talk, that is."

Jed shook his head, but he was grinning. "You want to know what Carolyn said?"

"Do I?" said Zaf, not knowing.

"She said, and I quote, she will write up her report and, despite Zaf's abrupt departure, it's going to score very well."

Zaf grinned. "Celebration dance!"

"We've already done our celebration dance," said Parvani. "Do not bail on us again, Zaf." She punched him in the arm, playfully.

"We did well," Zaf said, still unable to believe it.

"Celebrations drinks are on you." Jed threw an arm round his shoulder.

CHAPTER FIFTY-FIVE

Bev Bakewell spooned roasted veg onto Zaf's plate and passed it to him across the small dining table. They were eating off the new cherry-red plates Diana had bought for her mum. Whether this would have any effect on Bev's portion sizes was yet to be seen.

"And Carolyn said our tour was innovative and unlike anything else on offer in London at the moment," Zaf told them.

"Well done, love," Bev replied.

"Hear hear," Diana added. "Does this mean your little group has come out on top? Not that such things matter."

Zaf shrugged. "Graduation is in two days' time. Apparently they make a little thing of it. You'll be there?"

"Sounds like a grand day out," Bev said, "but I don't usually travel that far west."

The Guild of Tourism was little more than four miles away and in the heart of the city Bev called home, but she suffered from a fiercely emotional connection to her native streets that meant travelling any distance out of the East End was viewed with deep scepticism. She was a cockney with a pathological distrust of anything from the non-cockney world. She'd even regarded a holiday to Southend-on-Sea down the Thames as a journey to 'foreign parts'.

"That is a shame," Zaf said. "They're actually holding the ceremony in the nave of St Paul's which is super cool."

"A bit of pomp to celebrate your induction into the fine and ancient tradition of tour-guiding," Diana said.

"Well, you'd better be there," Zaf replied. "I need some support. I asked my mum and sister if they wanted to come down but Connie's on nights this week and Mum feels nervous about travelling to London."

"Nothing wrong with London," Bev said. "A fine city and a safe one for those who don't stick their nose in trouble."

Zaf smiled. He reckoned the woman criticising someone else for not wishing to make a trip from Birmingham to London when she herself was loath to cross a few miles of the place was the pot calling the kettle black.

"I will be there," said Diana. "But I'm going to visit Morris Walker again that morning. I should be back in time."

"Prison visiting again so soon?" Bev said.

"This Marengo thing. I simply have to share it with him."

Zaf frowned. "Are you sure that's wise?"

Diana pulled back a little. "Do you disagree? Do you now doubt what you heard and saw?"

"No, no, not at all," he said. "I saw a woman in a hat and little fluffy Pomeranian and she was calling 'Marengo! Marengo!'. I'm more concerned that you discussing this with Morris now will give him false hope. He's been in prison for, what, seven years now?"

"That's right."

"What good is a seven-year-old alibi provided by an old

woman and a dog who might have met Morris in café for a few moments? What are the chances they'll remember him? What difference will that make to his sentence?"

Diana stabbed a roast potato and then put her fork down. "I have to try. He's my friend."

Bev grunted. "You're a fool to devote all this time and energy to a man who is clearly guilty–"

"Mother!"

"– but he is your friend and sometimes, in this world, there's no more important bond than that between friends."

Diana's smile was sad and wistful. She picked up the small tumbler of water beside her plate and raised it in a toast.

"To friends. And family. Wherever they are. No matter how annoying they are."

Zaf and Bev raised their glasses to join her.

The three of them might have been sat around a tiny table in a cramped flat. Diana might have lost her own flat to a selfish, grasping landlord. Zaf might be currently lodging in a hostel while his relationship with Alexsei was struggling over the potholes of life. Their jobs at Chartwell and Crouch might be increasingly unsafe as the assets were sold off, one by one. And yet, in that moment, Zaf could not help but feel he was a very lucky man.

Bev sipped her water and put her glass down. She stared at the trays of vegetables and meat clustered on the chopping board at the centre of the table.

"I've cooked too much food again, haven't I?" she said.

"Maybe," Diana replied.

CHAPTER FIFTY-SIX

Zaf stood in St Paul's churchyard, flapping his arms like a big black bird. Graduation day. Relief and sadness swirled inside him. He'd survived the Guild's crazy training, but he'd miss the camaraderie of Jed and Parvani.

The Guild had given them all graduation gowns. A dozen or more of them waited to head over to the Cathedral for the formal ceremony.

"Tomorrow will be weird," Zaf said. "Not coming here, I mean."

"Yes," Parvani replied. "We'll all stay in touch though, won't we?"

"Course we will," Jed said.

"What about Josephine's group? Do you think Adi and Sacha will keep in touch?" Zaf nodded towards their rivals. Only Josephine met his gaze; the other two looked miserable.

"Yeah, they'll form some sort of support group," Jed said. "They should get *We Survived Team Josephine* printed on t-shirts."

"Shush, they'll hear you," Parvani said.

Dr Blackthorn, their tutor, strode over from the Guild building.

"There will be people waiting for us inside. Let's go, everyone."

The graduates followed him up the path and past the security guard into the Cathedral. The nave was a vast space beneath the high dome. But more than fifty chairs had been set out in a way that didn't make them feel swamped by the grand location. A lectern and red carpet had been set up a short distance away. They had their own area within the Cathedral.

"This is kind of spectacular," Jed whispered. "Big glitzy venue. No expense spared."

"Not sure if Christopher Wren was aiming for 'glitzy' when he designed this place," Zaf replied.

"Also, the Guild of Tourism and St Paul's have had an ongoing arrangement for decades," Parvani whispered. "They get this place free for their graduation and other ceremonies. In return, the Guild historians offer their expertise on historical and archaeological matters in the Cathedral."

"I stand corrected. But it's gorgeous anyway."

Parvani waved at her family on the front row. "I'm going to sit with my family."

"Go," Jed said. Then his face lit up. "Ariadne has come to see me graduate."

Zaf scanned the crowd to see if Diana had arrived yet. Instead of spotting her, he saw another familiar figure. Newton Crombie sat a couple of seats down from Ariadne. It took Zaf a second or two to recognise the object perched on his knee.

Zaf hurried over. "Newton, Newton." He slid across the rows to join the Chartwell and Crouch driver. "It's lovely to see you but..." He gestured to the cat carrier on Newton's lap. "You brought Gus?"

"We wanted to help you celebrate your special day," Newton replied.

"And that's... lovely. But Gus? Do you remember what happened when you took Gus to the theatre for the afternoon?"

"Technically, he took himself. And this is different. Ariadne thinks it's perfectly reasonable."

Zaf looked at Ariadne, who gave him a mildly alarmed look. "I'm not sure I said anything of the sort."

"She didn't say it was a bad idea."

Inside his cat carrier, Gus seemed remarkably chilled out. But Zaf didn't like the way he was looking at the carrier door, as if considering how to break out.

"God in heaven, help us."

"That's the spirit." Jed found the whole thing very amusing.

Zaf plonked himself down next to Newton. At least here he could keep an eye on them. But where was Diana?

CHAPTER FIFTY-SEVEN

Diana left Wandsworth prison in a reflective mood. Visits to prison were never cheery. Regardless of what one thought of prison as a punishment, one couldn't come away from one without thinking how soul-crushing it was to be incarcerated.

During her chat with Morris, she was struck by the thought that perhaps Zaf had been right. To mention Zaf's 'Marengo incident' might have brought false hope to Morris and caused him even more heartache. But the number of Pomeranians in the world called Marengo had to be vanishingly small. That one encounter alone was evidence that Morris's alibi wasn't a complete fabrication. It was a piece of genuine hope.

She had promised Morris she would all but camp out in Sloane Square and wait for the woman to reappear. There had been an expression of hopefulness on Morris's face when she'd hugged him and said her goodbyes.

Now, on the leafy street outside the Victorian jail, she wondered how effective hanging around Sloane Square would be in pushing the investigation forward.

"You turn up everywhere, don't you?"

Diana looked round to see Detective Sergeant Quigley, waiting to cross the road.

"I'm only ever in one place at once," she replied. Where DCI Sugarbrook tolerated Diana's thoughts on all matters criminal and mysterious, Quigley seemed to regard Diana's presence as a personal affront.

"You here on business?" asked Quigley.

"Visiting an old, old friend."

Quigley was carrying a brown manila folder under her arm.

"Police business?" Diana asked.

"None of your business."

"Anything to do with Marek Bogacki? He was an inmate here, wasn't he?"

Quigley scowled. "You think the police or the justice system move slowly. But nothing moves slower than the prison service." She waggled the folder. "I decided to come over myself to get Bogacki's dental records."

Diana nodded. "You still need to formally identify the body?"

"Just a formality. We need to dot the 'i's et cetera, et cetera before we send his body off for cremation. You'd normally get the family to make a formal identification, but his sisters didn't seem inclined to make the journey from Poland."

"He had sisters?"

"Two of them. I don't think they were close. No interest in doing the decent thing. So, here I am, wasting my time, when they could have come over here and gone 'yep, that's him'. I mean, one fat old bloke is just like another, but at least that box would be ticked and—"

"Two sisters?" said Diana.

"Yes. Did you not hear?"

Things clicked in Diana's head.

"Oh, my."

Quigley frowned. "You all right? You've gone pale."

Diana swallowed. The thoughts were whirling.

"That's the answer," she whispered.

"What's the answer?"

"I know who killed Marek Bogacki."

Quigley's frown deepened. "Oh, no. You're not turning amateur sleuth on me."

"I *know* who killed Marek Bogacki." She looked at her watch. "And I know where they are, right now."

Quigley stared at her. "You're not making this up?"

Diana shook her head. "You have a car. How quickly can we get to St Paul's Cathedral?"

CHAPTER FIFTY-EIGHT

As Dr Samuel Blackthorn took to the little podium to address the assembled graduates, friends, family and Guild staff, a figure slipped into the seat next to Zaf.

"Alexsei!"

He was surprised, but wasn't sure he should have been. Things had been rocky and weird between them, but Zaf still wanted Alexsei in his life. And Zaf had mentioned the graduation ceremony to Alexsei, even if only via messenger, and his boyfriend's answer had been polite but unenthusiastic.

"Didn't know to expect you."

"And miss your big day?" Alexsei took Zaf's hand. Zaf felt warmth spread up his arm.

At the lectern, Dr Blackthorn was launching into what sounded like a much-repeated speech about the long and historic role of the Guild of Tourism and its connection to this most important of London's landmarks.

"Sorry I was cutting it fine," Alexsei whispered. "I had a meeting with Simeon De Montford at Shivdler Legal."

Zaf knew the name. They were the solicitors who had

tossed Diana out of her home. "What were you talking to them about?"

"About the house. About my father's ownership and my stewardship of the place. I realised something."

"Yes?"

"I have defended my father by attributing his actions to these faceless legal types. I have defended him by doing nothing."

There were things Zaf might have said at that moment, ways of softening Alexsei's self-criticism, but he forced himself to be quiet and let Alexsei speak.

"It was easiest for me to do nothing when Diana was evicted. I had my home. I had my money. I was never going to be the one to suffer."

On the podium, Dr Blackthorn was now delivering a potted history of the Cathedral. Beside him, Carolyn Desanti was trying surreptitiously to look at her watch.

"I think I needed to stand up for what I believe in, for who I believe in," Alexsei continued. "So I went to Simeon De Montford to have it out with him and then, in an unexpected turn of events, I ended up with my dad on speakerphone too."

"And?"

In his little cat carrier, Gus meowed, as though echoing the question.

"It was decided that, financially at least, it was time for me not only to stand up for what I believed in but to stand on my own two feet."

"Your dad cut you off?"

Alexsei smiled, and as his eyes met Zaf's, Zaf felt a tiny electric jolt run through him.

"No. I cut myself off. I'm no longer unofficial landlord of

the Eccleston Square house. Dad is no longer going to fund me in any way."

Zaf clutched Alexsei's hand more tightly. "That's crazy."

"No. It was long overdue. I'm happy. Honestly."

"And so," said Carolyn Desanti loudly, cutting through the trailing end of Dr Blackthorn's speech, "it is perhaps time that we turn from celebrating the Guild itself and start celebrating its latest batch of graduates..."

The certificates were about to be handed out. Zaf looked to the door, wondering if he might see Diana come in at that moment. He certainly didn't expect her to miss this. And then he realised there was someone else who was absent from the ceremony. He craned his neck and looked about.

Where was Georg?

CHAPTER FIFTY-NINE

DS Quigley drove at speed along the long Wandsworth Road, up past Vauxhall train station. The tour guide in Diana felt a momentary urge to give her favourite Vauxhall train station fact (a brilliant one about a thirteenth-century English mercenary and the Russian word for railway station) but now wasn't the time. They had a graduation to crash and a murderer to accuse.

Quigley turned along the South Bank then took Waterloo Bridge across the river. As she drove she called Sugarbrook, explaining everything to him. Diana listened on speakerphone; the detective chief inspector's thoughtful response told her they weren't dismissing her theory out of hand. Whether Sugarbrook would get to the Cathedral in time to meet them was yet to be seen.

They turned right, Quigley switching on her lights to get through the traffic on Aldwych and the Strand. She abandoned the car on a wide pavement on Ludgate Hill, just outside the Cathedral.

"You'd better be right about this," the DS said as Diana started a swift walk towards the Cathedral.

"Oh, I'm absolutely right about most of it," Diana replied. "Some details might have escaped me, but there is so much I know to be true."

They walked from Ludgate Hill into St Paul's churchyard.

"The ceremony will be underway," Diana said.

"And he'll definitely be there?"

"Yes... No."

She pointed. Ahead of them, a figure was emerging from the hostel next to the Guild. Georg Strandman, a heavy coat wrapped around his large frame, was carrying a bulky suitcase.

"Looks like he's planning on leaving," said Quigley.

Georg saw them approaching. His eyebrows rose in alarm, then he turned to walk further along the churchyard and towards Canon Alley.

"Mr Strandman!" Quigley shouted.

He ran. He was a big man with unwieldy luggage. Perhaps hoping to hide rather than outpace them, he cut sideways and dashed through the open entrance of the Cathedral.

Quigley ran after him and Diana hurried behind. It was no distance to the great arched doorway. Quigley disappeared to the left. Diana looked at the volunteer attendant at the door.

"The man with the suitcase...?"

The attendant was already pointing.

Diana ran into the Cathedral proper. There were some tourists about but she could see the graduation ceremony taking place beneath the dome. Carolyn Desanti stood at the microphone, saying something about "a group tour project that was simply transformative and unlike anything else we've seen before at the Guild..."

And there was Georg Strandman, doing a terrible job of keeping a low profile as he scuttled across the floor, pulling the suitcase behind him.

Diana set off after him.

"Someone stop that man!"

CHAPTER SIXTY

ZAF HEARD Diana's shout and looked round. She was moving at a near run across the nave towards him. Only then did he see Georg, dressed as if for a journey, trying to get away from her.

"Stop that man!" Diana shouted again.

A figure rushed to intercept Georg. Josephine, built like a rugby player, flew forward and bowled him off his feet. The suitcase flew off in a different direction, colliding with the podium and splitting open.

Silver plates, platters and tankards flashed and crashed onto the floor. Gus gave a violent meow. Half the audience were on their feet.

Zaf squeezed along the line to get to Diana.

She was puffing as she neared the podium. She might spend her days walking untold miles across the great city of London, but she was no longer in shape for running.

"You OK?" he said.

"Fine." She leaned on him.

DS Quigley was encouraging Josephine to get off Georg and checking the older man for injuries.

"Ladies and gentlemen," said Dr Blackthorn, taking over the microphone from the gobsmacked Carolyn, "if we can just have a bit of calm. We'll soon have this all sorted out."

"Georg Strandman," Quigley said, "I am arresting you for the murder of Marek Bogacki."

"No, no." Diana frowned. "You know that's not..."

She went over to Quigley to remonstrate. Zaf stopped by the silverware that had spilt all over the floor. They were, as he'd initially assumed, the display pieces from the Guild museum, items he'd seen Georg looking at before.

Diana and Quigley were arguing quietly. Zaf heard Quigley say, "...frankly, I don't understand half the things that come out of your mouth. We can sort this out at the station."

"What is going on?" demanded Carolyn. There was a wild and unsettled air about her, which was understandable given the excitement.

Diana approached the podium. "I really am sorry, everyone. Please, if you can just take your seats."

Quigley had handcuffed Georg and was now helping him sit up. Georg was hissing in pain and complaining about his knees. Josephine, very happy with her contribution to the situation, was apparently doing a victory lap of the Cathedral.

"Really, I can explain," Diana said to everyone. "If you give me a moment. This is all about the sad death that occurred in the hostel by the Guild last week."

The audience quietened. Dr Blackthorn passed Diana the microphone he was still holding. She looked at it in surprise.

"Oh, I suppose..." she said, then spoke into it. "Last week, a man died at the hostel, in the room now occupied by my young friend and colleague, Zaf, here. I'm Diana Bakewell by the way, tour guide and alumna of the Guild of Tourism. A fine institution. Zaf was one of the first people to come across the body.

He'd been poisoned, and he was soon identified as Marek Bogacki, a homeless man and a known burglar."

She paused, as if gathering her thoughts.

"The police had the problem of investigating the death of man whose recent history was mostly unknown. He was homeless, possibly friendless. He had few contacts that we knew of. His family consisted of two sisters back in Poland, so estranged from him that they weren't even willing to come over here to identify his body."

Diana smiled to herself. "I suppose investigating a murder is sometimes a little like a historical investigation or an archaeological dig. It's like the mudlarking that Ms Desanti does on the banks of the Thames. You're sifting through things that no one has looked at in years, hoping for a glimmer of truth, a sight of the treasure. Sorry, I'm going on. This murder is actually about treasure. The Ludgate Candlesticks."

She waved a hand across the nave. "If you've not seen them, they're on display here at St Paul's. Beautiful craftsmanship depicting the story of the Rich Man and Lazarus. If you don't know it, it's about the lives of two men who are essentially the same, but for the fact that one lived a life of comfort and indulgence and the other did not. I would say you could take a look at them here except, unfortunately, the ones on display at the Cathedral are fakes."

"I knew it," said Zaf.

"That's not possible," said DCI Sugarbrook, walking across from the main door. "We looked at the candlesticks. No one could have stolen them."

"Ah, but there are so many things about this mystery that are 'not possible'," Diana said. "The security chap, Mr Kambarzahi, was very keen to point out that no one could so much as touch the candlesticks without setting off an alarm. It would be impossible to steal them. Equally impossible was the fact that I saw Marek Bogacki moving around inside the hostel on the night he died, in fact at least two hours *after* he was supposedly dead. Impossible."

"You were mistaken," said Sugarbrook.

"Equally impossible," said Diana.

"Then someone moved the clock hands to fool you," said Zaf.

"Strange and unlikely, but not impossible," said Diana.

Zaf's gaze went to Dr Blackthorn to see if he was showing any signs of guilt.

"It slowly dawned on me," said Diana, "that even if he might have enemies, Marek was a man without the sort of enemies who would employ a method of getting rid of him as complicated as poisoning his dinner, and that perhaps, therefore, Marek was not the murderer's intended victim. Those thoughts crystallised in my mind when I saw Georg Strandman looking quite out of sorts at the alumni dinner the other week."

Georg, looking most unhappy at being handcuffed, threw a fierce questioning look at Diana.

"We were having a lovely candlelit dinner in the hall. Several delicious courses from the Guild kitchens. And Georg looked positively awful. I'm sorry, but you did. Pale and clammy and ill at ease. Turns out I was wrong about the cause, but the thought had lodged in my mind. What if Marek Bogacki had not been the intended victim? What if Georg Strandman was? They were both staying in the hostel that night, only two doors apart from one another. Could it be possible?"

"Does that make any more sense?" Zaf asked. "Georg is practically a stranger here too."

"He used to be a lecturer at the Guild."

"But he's been in Egypt for the last ten years and it's been even longer since anyone here could have known him. Who in London knows Georg and would want to murder him?"

"No one," said Diana. "That's exactly the point. No one knew Georg Strandman and yet someone very much wanted to murder him."

CHAPTER SIXTY-ONE

DCI Sugarbrook huffed. "Make sense, Miss Bakewell, and quickly. We need to question Mr Strandman about that stolen silverware."

"But I want to hear what she has to say," said Dr Blackthorn.

Jed and Parvani murmured their agreement.

"To be clear," said Diana. "Georg Strandman will not be answering your questions. Not now, not ever. The murderer didn't target Georg because he knew him. He targeted him because of something Georg knew. The moment Georg saw the Ludgate Candlesticks here in the Cathedral, he would recognise that they were fakes."

Sugarbrook frowned. "The man couldn't tell if they were real or not, but he thought they looked right enough."

Diana pointed at Georg. "That man? No, not that man. He knows nothing."

A thought struck Zaf. The thought that Georg might 'know nothing'. Comments Parvani had been making throughout the entire course.

"Oh, my goodness!" Zaf exclaimed. "That's not Georg Strandman! That's Marek Bogacki!"

Diana nodded. The man Zaf had only known as Georg didn't nod in agreement, but he said nothing to deny the allegation, either.

Sugarbrook looked like he wanted to disagree and shut the whole thing down. But every time he opened his mouth to argue, he stopped.

"A lot of impossible things become suddenly possible if this man is Marek Bogacki," said Diana. "The people at the homeless hostel told me Marek had become scared of fire following a house fire in his past. In that case, why would Marek Bogacki have had a lit candle in his room? Why would Georg look so queasy in a room packed with flaming candelabras? This is Marek, a man with a fear of open flames." She turned to the burglar. "And I must apologise to you, sir, for not being able to tell the difference between a Polish and an Estonian accent."

"Oh! The first day at school," said Zaf. "The first time you were brought before us. You asked the class 'Is anyone Estonian?' Like, why would you do that, except to work out if anyone might call you out on your accent or possibly your inability to speak Estonian?"

Marek Bogacki gave a small shrug, the smallest of acknowledgements.

"And throughout the course," Zaf continued, "Parvani kept moaning that you never really taught us anything. All your lessons were based around us telling you what we already knew and expanding on that."

"Told you!" called Parvani.

"Except when it came to Jack the Ripper and gangster stuff!" Jed added.

"This is incredible," said Carolyn Desanti. "Unbelievable."

"And it still doesn't make sense," Sugarbrook pointed out. "People had seen Georg Strandman and Marek Bogacki check into the hostel. He hadn't slipped in unnoticed. We found Marek Bogacki in his room. If the dead man was Georg Strandman, someone would have had to drag him along the corridor. He was not a small man. If this is Marek and he poisoned Georg to steal the candlesticks, then he'd have had to swap two rooms around. It doesn't add up."

"You are wrong on a number of details, dear Chief Inspector," said Diana. "Let's think about what happened that night. Georg Strandman ate a shepherd's pie laced with fragments of organophosphate. Nasty stuff, taken from the hazardous waste removed from the building. It would have attacked his nervous and respiratory systems.

"I imagine Marek Bogacki, two doors along, heard Georg cry for help in his final delirium. He ran the short distance along the corridor to help and found Georg either dead or dying."

She turned to Marek. "I don't know what your initial intentions might have been. Perhaps it would have seemed natural to notify the receptionist. Or perhaps you would have simply left the poor dead man, and gone back to your room, not knowing what to do."

"And then you saw the wallet," said Zaf. "Stuffed full of Egyptian money. Thousands of pounds. You mentioned that to me. It must have played on your mind. That's what made you decide to do what you did."

"I think Marek spent some time debating it," said Diana. "There was a body, a shocking thing. If he simply stole the money then the police might come looking for it, maybe even try to implicate Marek in the man's death. So he turned over all the possibilities. And he didn't want to do that in front of the dead man whose possessions, and history, he was considering stealing.

"So he stepped outside the room to thinking. *That* was at nine o'clock." She made eye contact with the police detectives. "I did see Marek Bogacki at nine p.m. from outside the Guild. Marek was alive then. It was Georg Strandman who was already dead. That's how the coroner's time of death and my version of events match."

"The man Diana saw and the dead man I saw in the morning were two different people," said Zaf.

"Hollow kings," said Diana.

"What?"

"As men get older, the differences between them grow less. Both Marek and Georg were fat, grey-haired and unshaven. Facially, I imagine they're nothing alike. Georg Strandman wore spectacles and Marek – the *one* thing we agreed about Marek Bogacki was that he wore an orange knitted hat. I saw a large, grey, older gentleman in an orange hat and Zaf did likewise. And that was enough."

She gestured at the folder Quigley had under her arm. "Dental records will show that the corpse is not that of Marek Bogacki."

CHAPTER SIXTY-TWO

"But moving the rooms," said Sugarbrook. "Dragging the corpse from one to another. No man alone could lift Georg's corpse."

"So it was a good thing for Marek that he didn't need to," Diana replied. "Easier to simply swap belongings. Marek took Georg's belongings and dumped them in his own room. He put his own rucksack, maybe not even emptied, in Georg's room. The only things Marek left were a candle of Egyptian frankincense and Georg's own copy of his book about the Ludgate Candlesticks. They'd been brushed away down the back of the dresser. Marek put his hat on the dead man's head and took Georg's glasses."

"You never look through your glasses," Zaf said to Marek. "You always look over them. You've never needed them. It's like poor Mrs Astrakhan."

"Who?"

"A woman Josephine dragged along with her group from the Disney shop. She was wearing a Disney hat."

"That's right!" Josephine called out. "Try to show me up."

"But it's easily done," Zaf said. "We assume someone belongs, someone has a certain identity, just because of little things like hats."

Sugarbrook shook his head. "The men were now in the wrong rooms."

Diana chuckled. "Like a cat in a box."

"A what? Mrs Astrakhan, cats? What do you mean?"

"I was sorting out packing boxes at the depot the other week and I was surprised when our cat, Gus, wasn't in the box I thought he was in. A bunch of boxes all alike can easily be mistaken for each other. A hostel where the computer booking system was temporarily abandoned during the renovations and everything was written down on poorly organised sheets of paper. It was easier to accept who was in which room based upon who you found where rather than study the records."

"And what would this Marek imposter be doing it all for?" asked Dr Blackman. "Did he think he could steal our valuables and get away with it by pretending to be a lecturer?"

"He didn't think like that," Zaf said. "Marek had stolen Georg's money, clothes and identity. Why not? If life had little left to offer Marek Bogacki, why not live out your final years as the respectable Georg Strandman. He had a wallet full of thousands in Egyptian notes. He didn't know that would only convert to like a hundred quid."

"Eighty quid," said Marek.

"But some money, some clothes. All he had to do was get up the next day, leave as if nothing had happened, and be on his way. Except as he came out, there we were, Parvani and me, helping with the dead man. And when he told us his name we went 'oh, you're our teacher. Come with us.' The next thing he knew, he'd been dragged over to the Guild and shoved in front of a class. Then the police were suddenly everywhere and maybe it felt safer to play along with the deception. And perhaps he started to enjoy being a respected teacher."

"Best teacher I ever had," Jed shouted out.

"You are very kind, Jed."

"Marek had leapt into the life of Georg Strandman," Diana said, "and he brought some people a lot of happiness. He had cast off his old life. Marek could die and be left behind. The only thing he didn't let go of was a photograph of his two sisters. Zaf and I saw that in his room the other day. A tiny keepsake, but one which we spotted. It seems Marek Bogacki's only crime in this whole affair was to take the identity of a dead man who no longer needed it and live a life that would have otherwise been closed to him."

"Well..." Zaf coughed and looked at the bag of stolen silver on the floor.

"And maybe that," Diana admitted.

"From the Guild's own museum," Carolyn said. "Scandalous."

"I did not steal it," Marek said.

"Really?" Quigley had a wry smile on her face.

Marek scowled. "I am saying nothing."

"Are you saying Marek didn't kill Georg?" Sugarbrook said.

"I am," Diana said. "The killer wanted to kill Georg and, although they didn't realise it for a long time, they succeeded. If I can make an educated guess, I would say they went to the Guild canteen and bought the shepherd's pie. They then went round to the hostel, knowing there were no functioning CCTV cameras in there due to the renovations and, adding a sprinkle of poison to the plate, delivered a welcome dinner to a very tired man who had just flown in from Cairo. How gratefully he would have received it, even if it had just been left outside his door. He'd just got into his room, possibly lit a candle to refresh the air, but was definitely preparing to go to bed. He ate it and, within a couple of hours, was dying from what is effectively a nerve agent."

"But the murderer didn't know they had succeeded," Zaf said.

"Exactly."

"A poisoned dinner was delivered to Georg Strandman but, by morning, it was being reported that Marek Bogacki had died."

"The murderer's mind must have been reeling. I hope it was with guilt as much as anything."

"And now they still had Georg Strandman on their hands, or at least, they thought they did. It could have taken weeks to work it out. And even then there was the fear that Marek, masquerading as Georg, might be the key to unravelling the crime at the heart. So what could they do? I'm making a wild guess now, but I wonder if Marek found that silverware in his room this morning with a note saying something like 'take this and leave or I tell the police who you really are.' A wild guess."

The look on Marek's face suggested she was not a million miles away from the truth.

"Oh, heck!" Zaf. "I know who did it."

Diana nodded. "It's the person who stole the Ludgate Candlesticks."

"We've already seen how tight the security is around the candlesticks," Quigley pointed out. "It's nearly impossible for a casual thief to steal them."

"Indeed," said Diana. "But the thief had already stolen them. Years ago. Twenty years ago, long before the current security systems were in place. I should think they'd stolen them and sold them off and the money from that theft, however much it was, is long gone."

"Who?" Sugarbrook demanded.

Diana turned and took Carolyn Desanti's hand. Carolyn shuddered at the touch and swallowed hard.

"Carolyn, you are a dear friend and I'm sorry it's come to this," Diana said, "but the truth has to come out. You stole the candlesticks and you murdered Georg Strandman, didn't you?"

CHAPTER SIXTY-THREE

Carolyn's face was ashen.

"I... I... didn't," she managed. "How could you?"

"I should have seen it sooner," Diana said. "You all but told me that night. I was so wrapped up in my own problems – small by comparison – I failed to see the hole you'd dug yourself into."

"I didn't tell you."

"Not in so many words. We were in your office surrounded by the paperwork of a Guild of Tourism that struggled year on year to balance the books." She turned to the audience. "A fine institution, nonetheless," she offered, before returning to Carolyn. "And then there's your own financial mess. As you said, mudlarking doesn't pay the bills. A messy divorce and poor sales of your mudlarking books. The years have not been easy."

"Hardly an admission of guilt."

"No," Diana nodded, "but then you said something odd. You said, 'life throws strange and terrible problems at us and sometime radical solutions are called for.' That's what you said."

"Circumstantial at best."

"And then I came to the hostel to tell the police what I'd seen and you were there, keen to get the police out again. When I said I'd seen something, you stayed by my side until I was out of the building. And when we had it confirmed that the dead man was supposedly Marek Bogacki, you lamented that a person should die so close to your place of work and 'for no reason'. 'For no reason.' At that moment, you believed you had somehow poisoned him. Killed him 'for no reason'."

"I just meant..."

"I know what you meant. Furthermore, we bumped into the real Marek there. He was keen to get to his room. Perhaps he was keen to grab his belongings, the identity and cash he'd stolen, and try to disappear. But you said to him, I remember clearly, that his teaching should be confined to group activities and only Samuel Blackthorn should do the history lessons in and around St Paul's. You were trying to keep him away from the candlesticks."

"But how could they have been stolen?" Sugarbrook said.

"The security man, Mr Kambarzahi, gave us the vital information," Diana replied. "The candlesticks were removed for analysis twenty years ago. And, as he said, the team from the Guild of Tourism helped with that. The team. Carolyn Desanti among them. Carolyn, do you want to tell us how you did it?"

Carolyn looked away, her eyes brimming with tears.

"Some historical analysis," Diana said. "Some time alone with the candlesticks. That would have been sufficient for Carolyn to make impressions she could use to forge copies. And then she had all the time in the world to sell the real items onto the more unsavoury sort of antiquities dealer she might have known through her work. That could have provided her with the money she needed. The crime being covered up is two decades old."

"And there's another thing." Zaf bent and picked up one of the silver platters Marek had tried to make off with. "I saw Ms Desanti and Georg – I mean, Marek – in the little museum inside the Guild the other day. Carolyn, you asked Georg if he remembered these sixteenth century pieces he'd helped catalogue." He ran a finger over the 'VR' engraved on the platter. "This is Victorian. You were testing him – or rather, proving that you knew he wasn't who he said he was."

Carolyn pressed her lips together. The silent tears were falling now.

"And now that I think about it," Zaf said, "you told him how much the silver was worth and how poorly protected it was. You weren't just testing him. You were buying his silence, even if he didn't know that was what you were doing at the time. You wanted him to take the silver and run, vanish completely, as you'd wanted the real Georg Strandman to do."

"The sad and crazy thing is," Diana said, "even if the candlesticks had been discovered to be forgeries, you'd have probably had more chance of getting away with your original crime if you'd done nothing at all."

Carolyn's face twisted with self-pity. She snatched her hand away from Diana. "Oh, that's the curse of being a historian. You don't know what it was like there at the time, the decisions one had to make in the moment."

"Come now, Ms Desanti," said DCI Sugarbrook. "I think we might need to continue this conversation down at the station. Mr Bogacki can join us too."

"Goodbye, my students!" Marek Bogacki called cheerfully as he was led away. "It was, most definitely, an education."

Diana and Zaf watched the two detectives, their suspects and the bag of silverware depart the Cathedral. Seeing his two colleagues taken away, Dr Blackthorn returned awkwardly to the podium and took the microphone from Diana.

"I suppose," he said, "we still have some graduation certificates to hand out..."

CHAPTER SIXTY-FOUR

ZAF WALKED side by side with Alexsei from the Cathedral.

An arm came round and grabbed Zaf affectionately around the neck.

"I've not been to many graduation ceremonies," Jed said, "but that has to be the best one ever."

"I told you I didn't rate Georg as a teacher," Parvani said, close behind.

"Very much like Diana to upstage proceedings and make everything about her," Ariadne Webb observed.

"I must try to rein myself in," Diana replied, not rising to Ariadne's barbed words.

Parvani took hold of Jed and Zaf's hands, making a triangle of them.

"I'm going for a celebratory meal with the family. I suspect my graduation will not be the main topic of conversation. But we did it. Top scoring team."

"An absolutely killer team effort," Jed grinned.

"Doesn't count!" Josephine shouted from across St Paul's

churchyard. "Our teacher was a fake! All scores are null and void!"

"Ears like a hawk, that woman," Parvani said, astonished.

"Goodbye, Josephine!" Jed waved like a loon. "We love you!"

"That woman is very happy she got to rugby tackle someone inside St Paul's," said Zaf.

Parvani grinned, hugged her two fellow students tightly and then went off.

"Celebratory meal for us, too?" Jed said.

"Actually," Ariadne pointed out, casting noticeable glances first at Diana and then at Newton, who was carrying Gus in his little cat carrier, "some of us have proper, busy and fulfilling jobs that we need to return to this afternoon. A little Magical Mystery Tour of Beatles London."

"Oh, really?" Diana said. "I was planning on launching something similar myself."

"Following in my footsteps again?" Ariadne clicked her fingers for Jed to accompany her.

Jed gave a wink and a wave to Zaf as he went.

"He's cute," said Alexsei.

"Really?" Zaf raised an eyebrow. "I hadn't noticed."

"I might need to hang onto you more tightly."

Zaf smiled. "I'm going nowhere."

"So." Diana fell into step beside Newton. "Talk me through your thinking about bringing Gus to the graduation ceremony."

"It's nice for him to get out and about," said Newton.

"One loose latch and that cat would have been all over the place," she said. "He'd have been halfway up the liturgical banners on the wall or yowling from the top of the dome."

"I should think if he wanted to do that, the absence of a

loose latch wouldn't stop him," replied Newton. "He is his own cat."

"So you've not brought him out to prevent him passing himself off as a new cat and over-eating on other people's tuna?"

"Didn't work for Marek Bogacki in the end, if I understood correctly," added Alexsei.

"Oh, I think Marek – or Georg, as I'll always think of him," said Zaf, "enjoyed life in whatever way he could. I think he loved being Georg, for however little time it lasted."

"Enjoying life in whatever way we can is not a terrible philosophy," said Diana.

Newton turned to her. "This from the woman who has lost her home. Forced to live with her mum. And, the way things are being sold off, likely to be out of a job before the year is through."

"Indeed," said Diana. "So let's enjoy it all while we can."

Alexsei looped his arm through Zaf's and pulled him close. "I thought I might spend the afternoon flat hunting. Somewhere cool and modern overlooking the Thames, I thought."

Zaf gave him a look. "Your dad's cut you off, remember. Or you've cut yourself off. Same difference."

Alexsei smiled. His smiles were rare and handsome things.

"I might be cut off, but that doesn't mean I haven't been building up my own savings over the years."

"Oh, you're filthy rich, are you?" Zaf, playfully.

Alexsei winked. "Not filthy. But rich enough."

"Flat hunting it is, then. And you, Diana?"

Diana stopped and looked around. The sun was high over the magnificent dome of the Cathedral, the mother church for the city of London.

"I think I might take a stroll up to Sloane Square and the

Kings Road. I might see if I can see a woman in a hat with a little dog called Marengo."

Zaf laughed. "And win Morris's freedom? You think you'll succeed?"

"You never know."

Zaf couldn't help but be touched by her optimism. "You live in hope, don't you?"

"Always."

Thank you for reading *Death at St Paul's Cathedral*, the story will continue in *Death at Abbey Road*.

READ A FREE STORY, GUS THE THEATRE CAT

Gus the tabby cat is now a firm fixture at Chartwell and Crouch Bus Tours. Newton the bus driver has taken him under his wing and regularly provides him with cans of tuna. And the tour guides Diana and Zaf are finding he's a hit with the guests.

But then when Diana and Zaf are showing a group of theatre professionals around London, Gus disappears in a West End theatre.

Newton is distraught. He's searched the theatre high and low but can't find his beloved feline friend.

One night, when Diana and Zaf are watching the performance, he has a plan. It involves plenty of cunning, a fair amount of sneaking around in the auditorium and quite a lot of tinned tuna.

Can Newton find Gus without causing total chaos for the audience?

Find out in this London Cosy Mysteries short story.

Read *Gus the Theatre Cat* for FREE at rachelmclean.com/gus.

READ THE LONDON COSY MYSTERIES SERIES

Death at Westminster

Death in the West End

Death at Tower Bridge

Death on the Thames

Death at St Paul's Cathedral

Death at Abbey Road

Buy from book retailers or via the Rachel McLean website.

ALSO BY MILLIE RAVENSWORTH

The Cozy Craft Mysteries – Buy now in ebook and paperback

The Wonderland Murders

The Painted Lobster Murders

The Sequinned Cape Murders

The Swan Dress Murders

The Tie-Dyed Kaftan Murders

The Scarecrow Murders

Printed in Great Britain
by Amazon